For *On the*

"Clever and creative with lots of twists, tense moments and a perfectly balanced structure. . . . *On the Steel Breeze* is Reynolds in top form."
—*SF Book*

"For SF fans, the possibilities and imagination that has gone into the book will remind them of the heady days of Asimov and Clarke, of an age where imagination and people were more important in telling the story of humanity and guessing about its future."
—*British Fantasy Society*

"Few SF writers merge rousing adventure with advanced futuristic technology as skillfully as Alastair Reynolds."
—*Toronto Star*

For *Pushing Ice*

". . . he has a genius for big-concept SF and fans of Arthur C. Clarke's *Rendezvous with Rama* and Larry Niven's *Ringworld* will love this novel."
—*Publishers Weekly*

"Alastair Reynolds, an astrophysicist and the author of six previous novels, including the critically acclaimed Revelation Space series (beginning with the title novel in 2000), has established a reputation as the purveyor of big ideas in science fiction, particularly in the space-opera genre."
—*Bookmarks Magazine*

Cover art copyright © 2015 Thomas Canty
Cover and interior design by Elizabeth Story
Author photo copyright © 2015 Barbara Bella

Tachyon Publications
1459 18th Street #139
San Francisco, CA 94107
(415) 285-5615
tachyon@tachyonpublications.com

www.tachyonpublications.com
smart science fiction & fantasy

Series Editor: Jacob Weisman
Editor: Marty Halpern
Project Editor: Jill Roberts

ISBN 13: 978-1-61696-193-0
ISBN 10: 1-61696-193-7

Printed in the United States of America by Worzalla

First edition: 2015
9 8 7 6 5 4 3 2 1

ALASTAIR REYNOLDS
SLOW BULLETS

Also by Alastair Reynolds

Novels

Revelation Space
Revelation Space (2000)
Chasm City (2001)
Redemption Ark (2002)
Absolution Gap (2003)
The Prefect (2007)

Poseidon's Children
Blue Remembered Earth (2012)
On the Steel Breeze (2013)
Poseidon's Wake (2015)

Other
Century Rain (2004)
Pushing Ice (2005)
House of Suns (2008)
Terminal World (2010)
Harvest of Time (2013)

Collections
Diamond Dogs, Turquoise Days (2003)
Zima Blue and Other Stories (2006)
Galactic North (2006)
Deep Navigation (2010)

Novellas
"Thousandth Night" (2005)
"The Six Directions of Space" (2007)
"Troika" (2010)

alastair reynolds

SLOW BULLETS

tachyon | san francisco

My mother had a fondness for poetry. When my sister died, but before the news of my own conscription, mother showed me passages from a work by Giresun. It was a poem called "Morning Flowers."

This was an illegal act.

Giresun was the official war poet for the Central Worlds. Her works were banned in the Peripheral Systems, considered propaganda. But Giresun had been famous before the war, and my mother had collected several of her anthologies. She was supposed to have handed these books in during one of the amnesties. My mother could not do that. One of them had been a gift from Vavarel, with an inscription in Vavarel's beautiful flowing hand.

My sister had always had better handwriting than me.

"Morning Flowers" was about death and remembrance. It was about accepting the death of a loved one while holding onto the bright thread of their life.

Giresun was a great comfort to me during that time. But I could never speak of her work beyond our home, and after my conscription I had no way of taking her poem with me. I tried to remember it, but even the few short verses of "Morning Flowers" were too much for me.

Eventually a ceasefire was declared.

Many ships skipped into orbit around a neutral planet called Wembere. The military and political leaders agreed to their complicated and contentious terms. Before solemn witnesses they used things called pens to make markings on a thin, skinlike substance called paper, using a material called ink. They had been ending wars this way for thousands of years.

You will have to take my word about these things.

There was a problem, though. The skipships were the only way to send messages at faster than light speeds, so it took time for the news to spread. To begin with, not everyone believed that the ceasefire was real. Even when neutral peacekeepers came in to our system, the fighting continued.

Near the end of things I was on one of these patrols when I ended up separated from my unit. I was trying to re-establish communications and work out how to get back into our sector when I ran into an enemy sweep squad.

There were four of them: Orvin and three of his soldiers.

I knew a little about Orvin, even then. I had heard stories about this man who operated under the enemy's flag but broke even their rules of war. It was said that when the ceasefire came, both sides would be lining up to put him to trial. He caught me, and took me to the bunker. It was a low, armoured building that had been blasted and abandoned. It was cold and full of rubble, there was no glass in the windows. A mottling of dark red blood on the walls and floor showed where Orvin had already killed people.

His three soldiers held me down on a metal-framed bed that smelled of piss and death. Orvin used a knife to cut a gash in my trousers, running from the knee to the upper thigh. I tried to thrash and kick, but the soldiers were much too strong.

"Hold her down," Orvin said.

He was a big man, taller and broader than any soldier in my unit. His skin was the colour and texture of meat. His face also seemed too small for his head. It was as if his eyes and nose and mouth were not quite in proportion to the rest of him, a too-small mask. He had white hair, cropped close to his scalp, and white eyebrows. The hair and eyebrows stood out strongly against the meat-colour of his skin.

He had a trolley next to him. Very delicately he put the knife down onto the trolley. He had huge pink hands. His nail-less fingers were so thick and stubby that it made his hands seem babyish.

"Haven't you heard?" I asked, feeling the urge to say something. "It's over. Peacekeepers are here. We're not enemies now."

He produced from a lower shelf of the trolley a copy of the Book. It was a black rectangle, full of sheets of material like the paper I mentioned earlier, only much thinner. They had been marked with ink, but done using a machine rather than a pen. From the scuffed cover, I recognised the Book as the one that had been issued to me.

"Do you believe this?" Orvin asked.

"No."

"They say all you Peripherals read the Book." He paged through the Book, having trouble turning the pages with his thick fingers. "We have our own Book, too. For the most part our people are too educated to attach any significance to its contents."

"Not what I heard."

It was a risk, arguing with this man. But agreeing with him would have brought no favours.

Orvin began to tear pages out of the Book. They detached too easily, the way wings come off an insect. He crushed them up between his fingers and dropped them to the floor. He moved his leg as if mashing his boot on the pages.

"It won't work," I said. "You can't provoke me like that. I'm not a believer."

"Then we've that much in common," Orvin conceded, allowing the Book to drop from his baby fingers, onto the rubble.

He returned his attention to the trolley, moving his hand through different items. I thought for a moment he was going to pick up the knife again, but instead he came up with a thing shaped like a gun. It was made of white-coloured metal and seemed heavy in his hands.

It had a large trigger, with a hose running to a pressurised reservoir.

Orvin ran his hand along the barrel of the thing.

"You know what this is?"

"Yes."

"I know your name is Scurelya Timsuk Shunde," Orvin went on. "I pulled your data from your slow bullet. Where you were born. Your family. That odd business with your conscription. Your subsequent military history. The skips that brought you to this system. The times you were hurt."

"Then you don't need me to say anything."

Orvin smiled tightly. "Do you remember when they put the bullet into you?"

"I'm a soldier. Who doesn't remember?"

He gave a little nod of sympathy. "Yes, we used them on our side as well, or a virtually identical technology." He made sure I got a good look at the gun-shaped thing. "There's a slow bullet in this injector, programmed and ready for insertion."

"Thanks, but I already have one."

"I know that."

"Then you should also know about the transponder signal. My side will be zeroing in on it as we speak."

"I could always cut the bullet out before they get here," Orvin said.

"And kill me in the process."

"That's true. And you're right—there wouldn't be any point putting a *second* slow bullet into you. This one's had a few alterations, though. Shall I tell you what they are?"

"Go fuck yourself."

"Normally there's not much pain. The military medics use a topical anaesthetic to numb the entry area, and the slow bullet puts out another type of drug as it travels through your insides. It goes very slowly, too—or at least it's *meant* to. Hence the name, of course. And it avoids damaging any vital organs or circulatory structures as it progresses to its destination, deep enough inside your chest that it can't be removed without complicated surgery. But this one's different. It's going to hurt like the worst thing you've ever known and it's going to keep burrowing through you until it reaches your heart."

"Why?"

Orvin let out a little laugh. "Why not?"

I tried to fight—I had no control over that—but I always knew it was useless. The soldiers had me held down too well. Orvin leaned in and pressed the nozzle of the injector against the skin of my thigh where he had already cut away my trousers. I watched his hand tighten on the trigger, and heard a sound like a single whip crack. It was the air going through the gun.

The bullet entered me. It felt like a hammer blow. The gun made a sort of slow, satisfied sigh as the air went out of it.

For a second, maybe less, the pain was less than I had feared. Then it hit, and I screamed. It was what they had been wanting, and I hated myself for it, but there was nothing I could do about that.

"Can you feel it in you?"

Orvin pulled the injector away and cleaned the end of it on a scrap of rag. He put the gun down on the trolley.

"Fuck you." I said.

"This is just the start, Scurelya. In an hour or two it'll hurt much more than this. By then, you'll be begging for me to make the bullet explode, so that it kills you instantly."

"They'll find out," I said, fighting hard to get the words out. "They'll find out and find you."

"Oh, I don't think so. It's a big universe out there. Lots of systems, lots of chaos and confusion. I have my plans."

Where the bullet had gone in was a small hole, no wider than my little finger. I could feel the bullet moving itself, contracting and extending like a mechanical maggot. A little bump in my skin signalled where the bullet was pushing through underneath.

I was certain as I could be that I was going to die in that place. It would either happen when the bullet reached my heart (or some other vital part of me) or when I managed to persuade Orvin to make the bullet explode, as all the bullets were capable of doing. If it blew up now, it would probably take my leg off and leave the rest of me alive, at least for a while.

Obviously I did not die in the bunker.

If you have seen the drawings of me (they are not very lifelike, but they did their best) you will know that I did not lose my leg, or any part of my body. I may not be pretty, but all of me is there.

What happened was this.

There was a noise, some kind of air transport passing slowly overhead. I thought it might be soldiers of the Peripheral Systems coming to extract me (if I was worth that much trouble) or possibly the peacekeepers, or even Orvin's side looking for him.

Whatever the cause, it was enough to have Orvin break off from his entertainment and send one of his soldiers outside. Up near the top of one wall was a square hole where there might once have been a window or some kind of air circulator. I saw a machine cross the sky, then double back again. It was slowing down, making a louder sound than before.

"You're fucked now," I said.

Really, though, I did not know what to make of the transport, whether it was good or bad for me. I was in too much pain to think with any kind of clarity. All I knew was that Orvin seemed surprised by it, and I was glad to see him discomfited.

The soldier came back into the bunker and whispered something in Orvin's meat-coloured ear. Orvin scratched a hand across the bright white bristles of his scalp.

"We'll leave her," he decided.

"We could kill her now," one of the soldiers said.

"Now, an hour from now, it'll make no difference,"

Orvin said, speaking loudly enough for my benefit. "That transport isn't closing in on her transponder signal—if it was, it'd be much closer."

"You should kill me," I said.

"And why is that?"

"If you don't, I'll find you."

Orvin smiled at the emptiness of my threat. "See how far you get without a heartbeat. If you're really insistent, though, I will have that bullet detonate. Your choice."

"Fuck you," I said again. "And it's Scur. My name is Scur, not Scurelya. I want you to hold that in mind. I'll find you again, Orvin. I'll find you and make you remember this."

"Scur," he said, musing on the sound of it. "That's not a very nice name. It sounds like an insult, a word for a bodily function."

"It works for me."

They left quickly after that. For a minute or two I heard voices outside the building, but they soon left. There was no sound of a vehicle, or even the transport. But whatever it was had convinced Orvin to be on his way.

So it was just me on the piss-smelling bed.

They had not bothered tying me down. With the bullet in me they knew I stood no chance of catching up with them. They had also not left me with any sort of weapon or communications device. They had every reason to assume that I would be dead by the time anyone found the bunker.

They were wrong about me.

I waited until I was certain they were gone. Then I tried to move. It was hard because of the pain in my leg, and at first all I could do was whimper against the agony. Then I tried curling into a ball, hoping that would make it more bearable. When that failed, I slumped back onto the bed in despair and exhaustion. The bullet was still maggoting its way up the inside of my leg. I did not want to wait until it reached my pelvis.

I swung myself off the bed. I screamed with the movement but that actually seemed to help. I got both of my feet onto the rubble-strewn floor. They had taken my boots but I barely registered the cold or the sharp-edged things against my skin.

I propped myself up by my arms, able to get a much better look at my leg. The bump under my flesh had moved about half the distance to my upper thigh. I could measure its progress if I watched it against the hairs and blemishes on my skin.

My gaze settled on the trolley Orvin had been using. The injector was on it as well as all the sharp things. There was also the knife that Orvin had used to gash open my trousers. Next to the knife was a roll of surgical bandage, and next to that was a flask of disinfectant.

I thought of Orvin torturing people, but not wanting them to die of infection before he had had his enjoyment.

My attention returned to the moving bulge. I knew what I would have to do. Using the knife was going to hurt more than the bullet itself, and if I cut an artery I might end up killing myself anyway. Once I started, I would not want to continue. But I would have to force myself. The war was over and I wanted to get back to my old life, the planet where I had been born. I wanted to return to my mother and father, and let my father know that I did not blame him for my conscription. He had walked the hard path of the good and incorruptible man. He deserved better than to lose another daughter.

I took the knife and began to cut the bullet out of me.

— ✖ —

You know of the wakening. You either lived through it or you read of it in the other mandatory texts.

But we had no name for it then. It was a thing that happened to us in ones and twos, rather than a collective experience. And to begin with, none of us had the faintest idea where we were or what had happened.

I can only tell you how it was for me.

— ✠ —

After I pushed the knife into myself there was an interval of darkness, and then I woke somewhere. It was cold and there was no light. I imagined that I might have blacked out from the pain and come around again only a few minutes later.

But once I was able to assess my condition I realised that there was no longer any pain anywhere in my leg. I felt neither the bullet nor my wound.

I was still on a sort of bed but it was soft and it did not smell of piss. It felt as if it had been made for me, shaped exactly for the contours of my own body. I was thirsty, my throat uncomfortably dry, and I was cold enough to shiver. Wherever I was, it was not quite silent. From a distance I heard a sort of continuous low drone, like machines. Once in a while, as I lay there, I thought I heard a human voice.

I reached out and felt curving surfaces of metal and plastic. They enclosed me like an egg. My egg—what

I guessed must be a hibo capsule—made a sudden noise and opened itself. It came apart in two halves and a red light shone through the widening gap. The light must still have been dim but I had been in the dark long enough that I needed to squint.

I did not have my uniform or combat equipment on. Someone had dressed me in silver trousers and a silver top. The material felt strong and clean, but it was also very thin. The top had short sleeves and was done up with a simple sash around the middle. I felt as if it was the sort of thing a child or a sick person would be made to wear.

It was useless against the cold.

Gradually my eyes began to pick out more details of my surroundings. My capsule was one of many in a long, curving corridor. Of course you know these corridors for yourself. When I say "curving," I mean that it curved up and out of sight in both directions. On the opposite wall of the corridor lay another row of hibo capsules. It was not only mine that had come open in two halves: there were about a third of them already open. You may think I was instantly at home in the ship but it was not like that at all. I had travelled in skipships before, but I had never been awake for any part of the journey.

I could still hear sounds. Mostly it was the systems of the ship, churning away in the distance. But there were also voices coming from somewhere not too far away. The voices sounded as if they were having an argument.

I lifted up the fabric of my trouser. I made out the trace of the wound where the bullet had gone in and the place where I had cut it out. Or at least begun to cut it out—I could not be sure that I had succeeded by my own efforts. I ran my finger over the healed skin. It did not feel like scar tissue.

We had good medicine in those days. They could do anything, over and over again.

Still not quite trusting my leg—it would take my brain a little while to accept that it was healed—I began to walk along the up-curving corridor. It was an odd sensation to be walking up a slope that never stopped getting steeper.

You get used to it.

I passed many of the open and closed hibo capsules. There were still people in some of them—I saw their cold, still bodies through windows in the black shells of the egg. We were all wearing the same kind of silver clothes. I noticed also that writing glowed on the shells of the capsules. I paused to read some of it. The capsules all contained someone who had something to do with the war. The writing revealed what side they had been on, Central or Peripheral, and what their rank and service history had been.

I read the names of their homeworlds: places like Travnik or Yargora or Arbutax.

Supposedly we were being sent to Tottori, a place I certainly had heard of.

I needed to know more so I decided to find the voices. They seemed to be coming from further around the great curve of the wheel. I walked past capsule after capsule, noticing as I did that behind the capsules—half hidden by them—lay a series of gold and silver murals. Sometimes there was a picture of a stilt-legged bird or a building or a pleasant landscape. The black eggs had tubes and pipes coming out of them that went through holes in the wall.

The voices were coming closer and now they sounded much angrier. I heard the sound of some-one running, hard shoes clattering on the metal floor. I heard a sharp raised voice in an accent not like my own.

I squeezed into the space between two of the capsules and crouched down.

I risked a glance and saw a man coming around the curve of the corridor. As he ran, the man kept twisting around to look at the people coming after him. His black outfit looked much warmer than my own silver clothes. The man was very thin, with a bald, sharp-boned head. He wore boots and carried a small gun in his hand. He was about twenty paces ahead of a group of shoeless people all dressed in silver. There were women and men of various ages in the party. One of them held a hand to her forearm where it had been bloodied.

The man stopped at a part of the corridor where the walls squeezed in from either side. The man aimed his gun at the group.

"Get back!" he shouted, in a high, scared voice. "Get back or I will shoot!"

There were eight people after him. They had slowed but not stopped completely. Perhaps they doubted that the man really meant to shoot them again. The man aimed the gun and seemed to shoot past the group. The way his hand shook as he held the gun, the way he flinched at the blast, made me doubt that he had ever been a soldier.

I listened to the voices in the party. It was hard to be sure, but their accents sounded like the enemy to me.

The man touched a control in the wall where it squeezed in. A metal door slid across the width of the corridor. There was a small window in the door. The man stepped up to the glass and looked through, needing to stand on the tips of his toes.

I barely dared move. The people were hammering on the other side of the door and I saw a hand pressed against the glass.

The man still seemed tense to me. He touched a different control and leaned in to speak.

"This is Prad! I'm in wheel three. Where is everyone? We've got a breakout here! Dregs are awake!"

I heard the same words booming through the corridor, coming out of the walls at amplified volume.

Prad moved away from the door. He still had the little gun in his hand but now it was aimed at the floor. He wiped his other sleeve under his nose. He made me think of a rat. He was lean, frightened and unsure of himself.

Keeping very still, I waited until Prad was level with me. Then I sprang out as fast as I was able and threw myself at him. I knocked him off balance, sent him tumbling into the capsule on the other side of the corridor. I landed on top of him and twisted the little gun from his grip, the way you take a rattle from a child.

I sprung back onto my feet and levelled the weapon at Prad.

"Don't shoot," he pleaded.

My throat was still dry but I had to talk. "Who are you?"

"Prad. Service technician Pradser Hebel. I'm crew. Propulsion section. There's been a problem with the ship. A *serious* problem. We're drifting somewhere and there's been a power restart. None of you should be coming awake like this."

I did not care for any of this. I wanted certainty, authority, not more doubt.

"Tell me what ship this is."

"Skipship. Military transport. We're supposed to be on our way to Tottori."

"I know. What happens when we arrive—do we get to go home? Are we being repatriated?"

"No. Why would you think . . ." But then he thought better of that line of questioning. "No. Not repatriation, exactly. This isn't just a military transport. It's a prison ship. The *Caprice*. That was her old name; they just kept it after the refit."

"There's been a mistake."

"Most definitely."

"I mean, I'm a soldier, not a prisoner. I should not be on any military prison ship. I'm not a . . . what did you call those people? Dregs?"

"It's just a word. I'm sorry. I didn't think . . ."

I jabbed the weapon at him. "Who's operating this fucking thing?"

"Peacekeeper authority." He was still down on the ground and cowering. "Converted starliner. Used to carry passengers before the war, luxury end of the market. Hundred Worlds Circuit. Appropriated and outfitted for prisoner transport and civilian repatriation."

"The dreg run."

"I said I'm . . ."

"How big?"

He swallowed hard. "Very. Refitted for bulk capacity. Nearly a thousand sleeper berths."

"You said drifting. Are we close to Tottori?"

"I don't think so. We skipped, maybe more than once. It was a long haul, all of us in hibo, even the crew. Then this. Total power blackout. No idea how long it's been. Ship's coming back to life piece by piece." He swallowed again. "Staggered system recovery, to manage power consumption until all reactors are back to capacity." He looked at me with a sort of pleading desperation. "*That's all I know.* I've been trying to reach the rest of the crew, trying to find someone who knows more than I do."

"Get up."

"Please do not hurt me."

"I'm a soldier, not a criminal. I don't *hurt* civilians. Those other people. Why were they chasing you?"

He risked a shrug. "Like you, like me. Scared and not sure what is happening."

"I used to fight those people."

"When I ran into them they had already met five prisoners from your side. You're Peripheral, right?

There had been a fight. I think one man may have been killed." He was calming now, but he still had a very high, quavering voice. I began to think it was his natural register. "They've split apart now, bulkheads down, interlocks sealed. But there will be more trouble until we can get some kind of authority."

I looked at the little gun. It was the sort of weapon safe to use on a pressurised spacecraft. Low energy yield and a low cyclic fire rate. It would stop a person but not go through armour.

I doubted it would be much use against three people, let alone eight.

"Do you know there are other crew?"

"I hope so," Prad said.

"Hope so. But you've seen none of them."

Prad gave a twitch, confirming that this was correct.

"You said you were propulsion section. Does that mean you know how to operate this ship?"

"Some systems."

"So where were you hoping to get to?"

This ratty man looked at me with renewed fear, as if I might decide his fate on the basis of his answer.

"A control station," Prad said, with a tremble in his voice. "Not the main bridge. That's too far away. But I thought there might be more crew at the control station. Thought I might be able to see how bad the damage is and where we are."

"Then we should go there now. Show me the way."

"It's not too far from here. We have to use the elevator to go back up to the hub."

"Will we run into anyone?"

"I don't know."

A little way around the wheel was another door blocking the corridor. Prad looked through the window before making the door open. Beyond was another corridor flanked by the open and closed hibo capsules.

"Only crew can work these doors," Prad said. "It will buy some time."

Soon we came to a door set into the side of the corridor. I kept my attention on Prad as we went into the gold and silver elevator. I worried that he might overcome his fear and try to take back the gun from me. But Prad only pointed to a picture of the ship etched into a rectangle on one of the walls.

"This is where we are. Three centrifuge wheels along the spine, we're in the last of the three. That little light moving up the spoke, that is us." He blinked. "Are you definitely sure that you are not going to hurt me?"

"Tell me about the ship. Beginning with why you're so afraid of me."

Prad told me that the ship was one of hundreds being used to move people around at the end of the war. This was an unusual transport, though. It was not just prisoners. There were some ordinary soldiers and civilians among the frozen—innocent cases. But they had been put aboard just to bring the berths up to capacity.

"And the rest?"

"Difficult cases."

"Dregs."

Prad swallowed. "What they told us was, most of them were soldiers who'd committed acts against the laws of war. Crossing the line, exceeding sanctioned force. Whatever *that* means. The rest . . . I gather they're mostly worse. Traitors, mercenaries . . . civilian criminals. Rapists, murderers, black marketeers. A shipful of headaches, for the peacetime administrations. They would need to be put through courts, and people wanted quick justice."

"The worst of the worst."

"I suppose so."

"Fine. But this you need to understand. I am not one of them. I am—was—just a soldier. I didn't "exceed sanctioned force," or any of that crap. I just did my job, and got cut off from my patrol, and caught by the enemy. Nothing else. I shouldn't even have been conscripted."

"Then you were one of the soldiers who just happened to be carried aboard to make up numbers."

"Yes."

Prad started saying something, then caught himself.

"What?" I asked.

"Where you found me. That part of the wheel."

"Yes."

"Is that close to where you came out?"

I thought of how far I had walked since emerging from my egg. "Not far."

"Then it doesn't fit. That whole area . . . I spent enough time in it to read some of the histories on the hibo caskets. Those were the problem cases. That whole section was full of military prisoners, scheduled for war crimes tribunals."

"Then you're saying I'm lying?"

"No!" Prad said. "Just that something doesn't fit. Just that someone must have made a mistake."

"I am not lying."

"Then you were assigned to the wrong section of the ship." Then he touched his forehead. "Your bullet."

"What about it?"

"We can read it out, access your core history. It'll tell us what you were doing right up to the moment you were injured, and your subsequent medical treatment, and the reason you were put aboard."

"You mean, it will vindicate me."

"Yes," Prad said, a touch too hastily. But what he meant was, it would let him see if I was telling the truth or not.

Which might be the last thing he learned.

— ✳ —

When we stepped out we had much less gravity than before, since we were now much closer to the middle of the ship. I did not care for the sensation of being nearly weightless. It was only a little like swimming and my combat training brought no advantage in this unfamiliar environment.

Prad, by contrast, seemed much more at ease. He pushed himself out of the elevator on his fingertips and walked in long drifting arcs.

I kept my eyes on him.

"You're used to this."

"Should be. Served on this ship long enough."

"Long enough to remember life before the war?"

"None of us served on this ship during its civilian days, although I met a couple who did, back when I was starting out. They say it was very beautiful, when it worked the Hundred Worlds Circuit."

The control station was a large room shaped like a hexagon. In the middle was a console and some seats. The walls were covered in moving writing and numbers and drawings—you will have seen something of that, sometimes, but it was different in those days, when the ship remembered more of itself. I found it hypnotic, like listening to the purr of a dreaming cat.

Prad closed the door behind us.

"We should be safe for a while. If they start breaking through into this section, we shall know it in time to leave."

"You hope."

"I am just doing my best. By the way, I still don't know your name."

"Scur," I said, after a moment.

"Just that?"

"Yes. Just that."

Prad went to the console and showed me how it was possible to monitor any part of the ship from this station. He unclipped a slate from the console, cradling it in his right arm while he tapped instructions into it with his left. At first there were problems getting the slate to work properly, but after a few minutes Prad seemed to have found his way around the worst of the difficulties.

"Is that your only slate?"

"No, there are hundreds more on the ship. This is what we have to work with now, though."

He told the slate to display images onto the wall. I saw the wheel where I had come out of hibo. The corridor was empty but in another view there were a dozen or so people dressed in silver clothes and crowded around something. In another view people were trying to make one of the doors open. In another there was a woman dressed in silver running along a gold and silver corridor on her own.

In another a woman and a man in black clothes were talking to a girl wearing silver.

I remembered how cold it had been when I came out of the casket. It was no warmer now but at least I'd been moving around.

"She's just a child. What the hell are children doing on this ship?"

"There won't be many," Prad said. "They'd have been among the civilians."

"I'm worried for her."

"At least we know there are other crew. Enough of us and we can restore some sort of order."

"Against a thousand prisoners? Good luck with that."

"There won't be that many. I haven't been awake long, but I've already seen that we aren't at capacity. Not now, anyway."

"What does that mean?"

"Quite a lot of the hibo berths aren't working properly. They've failed. The people in them, they're . . . well, dead. Or as good as dead. They might be cold now, but if they've become too warm at any point in the trip, they'll have massive cell damage. All told, I doubt there are more than six hundred good units."

"Out of a thousand? Why would they just fail like that?"

"There's always that chance. Normal risk of space travel, even on a ship like this. On a long series of skips, across a year or two of flight, you might easily lose one, maybe two sleepers. But we've lost two hundred, three hundred people."

"So we've been out for more than a year or two."

"I suppose we must have."

"There has to be a way to find out. The ship has to have some record of how long it's been floating here."

"It will not be that straightforward. The blackout hit us pretty hard." He tilted the slate to me, as if I was expected to make sense of the figures and diagrams it was presently displaying. "Total reset. All clocks zeroed. Normally what would happen is . . ." But Prad trailed off. "Look, this is complicated. The ship has no idea where it is or how long it's been here. But that shouldn't matter. Normally it can always pick up an external beacon, reset its clocks and navigation systems."

"And?"

Prad tapped a finger against the slate. "It's not picking up a signal. Those are *zero return* error conditions. I've tried the console as well. It is most certainly not a local fault."

"Then we're out of range. Maybe we came out of skip at the wrong point."

"The NavNet's too extensive for that. Hundreds of thousands of beacons, massive system redundancy. Even during the war they managed to keep most of it still running. But there is nothing out there."

"Zero return," I said, echoing his earlier statement. It had an ominous, hollow quality to it.

"Well, there could be a fault somewhere. I know one thing, at least. We might be drifting, but we are not in deep space, far from any system. Before we met . . . I told you I was looking to find the rest of the crew. I thought the rings might be a good place to start, and I also wanted to make sure that the prisoners were still safe."

"For our welfare, or yours?"

"A bit of both. Anyway, I passed a window. There's a planet out there. If this slate was working properly I could call up an external view from in here."

"Did you recognise it?"

"No, and it's not Tottori either. Maybe another world in Tottori's system, but that's a heavily settled space and I saw no orbitals or stations or elevators, let alone any other space traffic."

"It has to have a name."

"I agree—it's somewhere, at any rate. Atmosphere, land masses and seas. Looks liveable, if a little on the cold side, so it's got to be somewhere *known*. Must still be off the beaten track, or we would not be the only ship here."

"Very off the beaten track." But I had seen something on the wall that bothered me. "That view. It just changed. Can you go back?"

"What was it?"

"People in a big room. For a second I . . ."

"What?"

"I thought I knew one of the faces."

Prad did frowning things with the slate until the view was back on the wall. It was one of the grand ballrooms of the old ship, a place with big windows and a curving floor like the corridor with the hibo caskets. Prad said it was in an area of one of the wheels given over to ballrooms and lounges and promenade decks.

There were about twenty-five or thirty people in this room and most of them wore the silver outfits of the prisoners. They were gathered around a pair of tables that had been pushed together, with a man in a silver uniform stretched out on his back on the table. He was being held down by his hands and feet.

"You're all wearing the same outfit now, so there's nothing to mark one side from the other. It's anyone's guess as to who came out of which hibo berth. But maybe you know some of these people?"

"No," I answered, before starting to say something.

"What?"

"It can't be right, but I thought there was a man in that party I recognised."

"Someone special to you?"

"Someone I'd quite like to skin alive, if I ever got the chance."

"Charming."

"Don't mock me, Prad. There was a man called Orvin, a war criminal operating for the enemy. He caught me, tortured me, left me for dead."

"And he's here?"

"I thought so for a moment. It was just a flash, his face on the wall. But if it was him, he has his back to us now."

"That big man there?"

"Yes." I thought of his meat-coloured skin, his brilliantly white hair. It fitted, but Orvin could not be the only man who looked something like that,

39

and it was not easy to judge his size against a group of strangers. "Can you get a different angle on him?"

"I think that's all we have. If we wait, he might turn around. Would you know if he did?"

"Yes."

But he did not, and meanwhile the group seemed to be doing crueller and crueller things to the man on the table. One of them had a silver tool in his hand, an instrument I recognised all too readily.

"What in the worlds is that doing here?"

"It's a slow bullet injector," Prad said, as if I might not have known the thing for what it was. "This is a military transport. Sometimes the bullets inside you aren't working properly, so we need to put another one in. It's normally done when you are asleep, being readied for hibo."

I thought back to my own time in the bunker. I said I would say nothing more about my life before the wakening, but it was hard to let this memory slip. I could still feel the hard, cold floor, the broken glass under my feet, the blood-spattered walls, the smell of piss and terror.

"They make good torture instruments as well."

"Perhaps you just saw a face."

"Perhaps I did." I was ready to believe that, even hoping that it was the case. "But they're going to kill that man if we don't do something."

Prad regarded the little gun I still held on him. "You think you can take that room? In which case, good luck with *that.*"

"There must be more weapons somewhere."

"There are, but nothing more powerful, and there are still only two of us."

"The thing you did earlier, speaking to the entire ship. I heard your voice. Can you make them hear us from in here?"

Prad nodded, and showed me something on the console. It was a stalk you bent around and spoke into. Prad said it was so the crew could address the passengers and staff in case of an emergency or drill. There was not much use for such a thing on a prison ship with frozen passengers and a skeleton crew but the system had never been disconnected.

Prad tested a few controls to make sure it was still working.

"What do you want to tell them?"

"That we'll destroy the ship from here. It'll sound better if you convince me we could actually do it."

"Destroy the ship," Prad repeated, as if I said something in a strange foreign language.

"Destroy it, or kill everyone aboard. Whichever's simpler. Can that be done?"

"I don't follow. Why would we want to *destroy the ship?*

"Because we will murder each other given the chance. We're soldiers, Prad. Enemy combatants—and that's the best of us!"

"And you think the thing to make peace is to threaten to destroy the ship?"

"I know soldiers, Prad. I am one. They aren't going to listen to reasoned persuasion—not while there's a chance to settle some grudges. If they feel the way I do, then it only seems like hours since we were fighting."

Prad told me it was hard to make a ship like this destroy itself. Every system was designed to prevent such a thing rather than make it more likely.

I would not give up that easily.

"Dump the air, or threaten to do it. There must be a way."

"No," Prad said. "There's no good reason why you'd ever want to do that. We could, manually, seal off every section one by one and run a pressure dump. But not from here, and not in anything less than hours."

"Then we make it too hot or cold. Or stop the wheels, so that everyone has to deal with weightlessness."

"Again, it would all take much too long, even if we could do it from here."

"It doesn't matter what we can and can't do. It's

what we can convince them we can do. You give me the words, I'll make them believe I mean it."

He shook his head. "I do not think it is possible."

I showed him the gun again, reminding him of the essential nature of our relationship. "I'm not going to wait for them to tear each other apart."

"So you would rather kill me first?"

"Just give me something that will work."

After a moment Prad said that he could make the ship put out an alarm signal that would be heard in all the corridors and rooms. The lights would flash and a siren would sound. It was part of the arrangements for an emergency drill but the soldiers would be none the wiser.

"Do it," I said.

Prad put down the slate and did something to the console. The alarm started up. It was a rising and falling wail, reminding me of an attack siren. Red lights had started flashing on the walls. On the displays we could see that the people in the rest of the ship were hearing the same alarm. They were looking around. Even the man with his back to the camera was twitching his head.

"Do you want to speak to them now?"

"Give it a minute or two. Be better that way."

It was a long couple of minutes until I leaned in and started addressing the ship.

"My name is Scur. I know you can hear me. I'm a soldier. Until the ceasefire I was fighting with the rest of you. I have no idea what I am doing on this ship or what has happened to it. But I know we're in some kind of trouble." I took a breath. I would have liked more time to think through my statement, but I would just have to do my best. "I'm with a member of the crew, a man called Prad. Prad's pretty jumpy about the whole situation. Says we should be picking up NavNet beacons, and we're not. Zero fucking returns. Says that there are a lot of frozen bodies in the hibo caskets—more than there should be, given how long we were supposed to be out here. Now Prad and I have control of some of the ship's systems. I have a gun on Prad and I've asked him to do something. What have I asked you to do, Prad?"

Prad leaned in. "Initiate a hypercore excursion. The hypercore is what we use to boost power prior to the skip. Unless dampeners are applied the core will become supercritical in four to five minutes. The core will detonate and the ship will . . . well, there won't *be* a ship."

"Did you get that, people? We're a ticking time bomb with a four- or five-minute fuse."

I had their attention, that much was obvious. It was not just the people in silver—the soldiers and dregs like me—but also the crew in their black clothes. No matter what Prad believed, it seemed to me that there were much less than twenty of them.

"I'm not a technician," I continued. "I know guns, not skipships. But we can't keep fighting. Unless it stops I won't allow Prad to make the core safe. There are three wheels on the *Caprice*. Counting from the front, those who fought for the Central Worlds will take the first wheel. Those who fought for the Peripheral Systems, take the next wheel along. The rest of you—crew, civilians, anyone who *wasn't* a soldier—you take the third wheel. Once you're there, decide who'll speak for you. I don't give a shit how you make that decision, so long as you pick one person."

"Less than four minutes," Prad said.

"You'd best get moving. Whoever you've caught, no matter what you think they deserve, you'll leave them where they are. No one touches a hair on anyone's head from now on."

I had not counted on them to just get up and do my bidding: no one is that naïve. To begin with, I fully expected them to doubt my sincerity. They knew they had a few minutes to think things over.

But I had more to say.

"Maybe you don't think I'm serious about this. Perhaps you don't think I'd give up my life to make a point. You're wrong. I was left to die before the ceasefire, left with a slow bullet eating its way to my heart. That changes your perspective a little. I don't feel that I've a lot to lose at this point. It's possible we've been out here for more than a few years. And guess what? If anyone was thinking of rescuing us, they'd be here already. That means it's down to us. If we're going to survive, then we need to cooperate. The ceasefire happened. There is no war now."

"Three minutes," Prad said.

They were not yet moving to the wheels. But I could sense their uneasiness. They were thinking about it, wondering how far I might go. Some of them were looking out of the rooms and corridors they were in. If one moved then more would follow.

I kept a particular eye on the man I thought might be Orvin. But he had yet to turn his front to me.

I decided not to overplay my hand by making a further statement. I touched a finger to my lips, telling Prad not to say anything, and at the right moment he held up two fingers, telling me how many minutes were left.

I wished now that I had saved the lights and the siren until after issuing my demand: it would have made more of an impression. But perhaps I had already made the best of things. It seemed to me that I had spoken the truth even as I lied. There was no chance of the ship destroying itself—unless Prad was lying to me—but I was entirely serious about not wanting to die by the terms of the mob.

They began to move. It started in ones and two and threes and then became a surge. Prad moved to silence the alarm but I stayed his hand. Let them continue to think that death was imminent.

"They're bound to run into each other on the way to the wheels," Prad whispered. "There'll be more trouble."

"Less than if they stayed where they are."

"You call that a solution?"

"The situation is still fucked. It's just slightly less fucked than it was a few minutes ago."

Of course I knew that this was a stopgap. Not all the soldiers would know where to go. Did a traitor or deserter go to wheel one or wheel two? Some of the civilians had probably done worse things than some of the soldiers. Their hatred for each other might be just as strong.

I could do nothing about that.

"I think they swallowed it," Prad said, shaking with relief.

I doubted that they had, but it was the result that counted. It might only be that moving to the wheels was the safest thing to do while there was still some uncertainty in their minds.

What mattered was that I had established a starting point. The ship was emptier now and the worst enmities contained in the wheels.

Also, I knew I'd been right about Orvin. I had caught enough of a glimpse of his face as he turned to leave the room.

He walked among us.

— ✕ —

It took time for the people in the rings to sort out their lesser differences and agree on three representatives. During that time—whether it was an hour or six hours—Prad made further investigations into our condition.

This much we knew:

Caprice had suffered some kind of blackout and was now struggling to restore all its systems. Of the thousand or so hibo sleepers who had been aboard when the ship started its journey, two hundred and forty had not survived the trip. Huge areas of the ship were still dark or suffering intermittent power drops. This was bad, but there was good news as well. The ship could provide and recycle enough water and food to keep all of us alive indefinitely, so long as we accepted a system of rationing. It would not be comfortable, but none of us need starve. Equally, we had power enough to keep warm. There were no beds or private quarters on this prison ship, except for those reserved for the crew. But there were hundreds of spare prison garments, and these could be fashioned into rudimentary bedding. Some of us curled up back in the hibo berths, which offered a measure of privacy. Others chose the protection of communal sleeping arrangements. So we could eat and sleep, wash ourselves and remain warm. As soldiers, most of us had put up with worse.

But we knew nothing about our larger predicament. The ship's electronic nervous system was only partially functional. It was blind to areas of itself, and blind to a great deal of the outside universe.

And yet, it had managed to limp into orbit around a world. The orbit was high and stable—far enough above the atmosphere that it could be maintained almost indefinitely, with only tiny automatic thrust adjustments needed every few decades or so.

Could we have been here that long?

Prad thought he might have a way of determining where and when we were, independently of the NavNet. In his early investigations he had tried varying the search frequency in case—for some reason—the NavNet transmission protocol had been altered. He had been excited when the ship began picking up a regular radio signal, similar to the positioning pulse from a NavNet beacon.

But the signal was natural in origin. Prad quickly realised that it was coming from a radio pulsar, the dense, rapidly spinning magnetic remnant of an exploded star.

But that gave Prad a better idea. There were thousands of radio pulsars in the galaxy and they were all rotating at different speeds. The strengths of those pulsars would depend on how far away they were. By triangulating off these natural signals it should be possible to work out where *Caprice* had ended up. It would not give us as good a fix as the NavNet but it would be sufficient to determine which solar system we were in.

Prad said to me that he could do better than just a positional estimate. Since all the pulsars were slowly winding down, it should also be possible to estimate how many months or years had passed.

I told Prad that I should be extremely interested in the answer.

— ✻ —

The representatives were called Yesli, Spry and Crowl. I met them in a lounge near the control station. They were all among the older people in their respective wheels, if not the very oldest.

I knew none of these people before the wakening, so I had no sense of whether I could really trust them. Equally, I had no choice not to proceed as if they were completely sincere. These were the figureheads that the wheels had selected, and that was an end to it.

Yesli was the only woman among the three, and she was the civilian representative of the third wheel, the one that contained the noncombatants and those who had no place in the other two wheels. She was older than me, from a different world—a different solar system, in fact—and she had a measured, cautious way of speaking.

I thought I liked Yesli, at least to begin with. She could be very persuasive, but it was as if she knew the power of her own words too well. She did not need to say much to have the attention of those around her, and this was a gift she used wisely.

Yesli had lost most of her family during the war and had reasons to dislike both sides. By the same token she had no strong reason to favour one side over the other.

"You know who I am now," Yesli said, when she finished telling us who she was. "What about *you*, Scur? We've been elected, the three of us. As far as I can tell, you just decided to put yourself in charge."

"It's a fair point," said Spry, who was a tall, shaven-headed man with very prominent cheekbones. He had muscular forearms which he liked to fold across his chest. "We've been selected by a sort of democracy, if you can call it that. I never asked to be placed in a position of authority."

"But you didn't turn it down, either," Crowl said, with a half smile. He was a small, unimposing man who looked no one's idea of a soldier, much less a natural leader. But there was a cleverness in his eyes, a confidence in his manner, that had evidently won people over. Of all us he was the most relaxed in this low-gravity section of the ship. "Neither did I," he went on. "As far as I can tell, Scur did the only thing open to her. If she hadn't, we'd be drowning in our own blood by now."

"Scur's another soldier," Yesli said. "It doesn't surprise me that you'd defend her. Frankly, I don't see why soldiers should have any say on this ship at all."

"Civilians are in the minority," I pointed out.

"And this is not a military situation. This is not a state of war. We're at peace. There was a ceasefire."

"Fine," Crowl shrugged. "Then we're all civilians now."

"Except for the war criminals," Yesli said. "The . . . what did they call them, these people?"

"Dregs," I said, smiling nicely.

"I'm one of those dregs," Spry said, surprising all of us with his frankness. "I'm perfectly happy to admit it. During the war I served under a superior officer who committed numerous acts against the laws of war. She executed soldiers without due regard for military process. She murdered civilians. So I killed her, and a number of the men and women protecting her. That makes me a military criminal, by the laws of my own side. A traitor and a murderer."

"Do you regret what you did?" I asked.

"Only that I didn't act sooner, and that I didn't take down a few more of the fuckers while I was at it. I regret that I allowed some of them a relatively painless death."

I decided that I liked Spry's honest absence of contrition. I should have found it much harder to trust him if he had produced a show of remorse.

"So it's not all black and white," I said. "There will be good and bad in all of us."

"And you?" Yesli asked. "What are your particular misdeeds, Scur?"

"You tell me. I'm a conscripted soldier who obeyed orders, did her job, and just happened to end up on this ship for no reason that I can understand."

Yesli nodded carefully. "Then you committed no criminal acts? Nothing against the laws of war?"

"I think I just told you that."

"Yesli has a point," Spry said, conciliatorily. "It would be good to know your intentions, Scur. It's not that we don't necessarily trust you, but you can't deny that you *did* seize power by threatening an innocent member of the crew."

"Who was running from a mob about to tear him limb from limb," I replied.

Spry nodded. "All the same."

"I used the gun to make my point. But Prad understands that it wasn't personal. You're right to ask, though—all of you. What *do* I want? The truth is, I have no intention of running this ship. You can sort that out between yourselves, just as soon as Prad comes up with a positional fix and an idea of how long we've been out here. I just want to see that we have a chance of getting home, whatever long that might take." I paused. "And I have some unfinished business I'd like to attend to."

"Business?" Yesli asked sceptically.

"There's a man on this ship I'd like to meet. I saw him on one of the screens, before I forced everyone to go back to the wheels. After that, with everyone moving around, it was hard to trace his movements. I think he knew that, and used the confusion to his advantage. But he can only be in one of the three wheels, and he's wearing the same silver outfit as the rest of us, rather than the black of crew. I know him as Orvin, although that might not be the name he's using now. But he won't be hard to locate. He's a very big man, with very white hair, and he has a face that makes him look like a baby."

"Who is he?" Spry asked.

"A true war criminal, unlike yourself. He and I have some history. We were on the same planet together, when the ceasefire came down. He did something bad to me, and now I'd like to put things straight."

"You mean," Crowl said, "that you'd like your revenge."

I looked at him, gave every impression that I was thinking things over before answering.

"Yes."

I don't think it was the thing any of them were expecting.

"I thought the time for lynch mobs was over," Yesli said.

"They are," I said, nodding. "There won't be a mob involved. Just me and Orvin and maybe something sharp. Once I have him, once I've settled our particular debt, the ship is yours. Run it as a trinity. Run it as a dictatorship. Organise yourselves however the fuck you like. I don't care. I just want Orvin, and some time alone with him."

Spry had his muscular arms still folded. "How do you propose to proceed?"

"Seal off the wheels for the time being. The three of you return and organise search parties with whoever you feel you can trust. Then start going through your people, one by one. Anyone you think looks the part, anyone you even have the slightest doubt over, you isolate them until I can check them out for myself. I won't need to be there. Prad can help me use the cameras."

"Will Orvin know that you're looking for him?" Yesli asked.

"I made a mistake, announcing myself as Scur. He knows my name, and I imagine he remembers leaving me for dead."

"It's an unusual name," Spry admitted.

"I don't like this," Yesli said.

"I don't either. But I like the idea of Orvin being among us even less."

I turned around sharply, aware of Prad making his way toward us along the corridor from the control station. I knew instantly that something was wrong, just from the look on his face.

I started to ask him what was amiss.

Prad halted. He looked terribly ill. I think if he had had anything in his guts just then, he would have vomited.

It was not illness, though. I had seen people in the war look this way, when they had witnessed something that no decent person should ever have to see. It was usually the realisation that we are just fragile bags of meat and bone and blood, held together by almost nothing. With Prad it was a different sort of realisation, but no less discomforting.

"Prad," I said.

"I can't . . ." he started to say.

"Prad, talk to me."

But all Prad could say was that he was sorry, over and over again.

— ✖ —

Yesli, Spry and Crowl followed Prad and me back to the control station. It seemed to me that Prad was still on the verge of hysteria. "There's been a mistake," I said, trying to calm him down. "Whatever you think you've discovered, it can't be as terrible as it seems. You're like the rest of us—not at your best."

I was doing what I had done in the war—trying to shake someone out of the paralysis of shock and fear, so that they could move and react and continue the business of not dying.

"You don't understand, Scur. There's been no mistake."

"Talk to us. Tell us what you've found."

"It won't make any difference, knowing."

"Tell us!" I snarled.

By turns he found some measure of composure. It took a while. Prad was not a soldier, and shock was not something he could just put behind himself for the sake of survival.

But it helped that he had to explain a technical matter to the rest of us. It was like a prayer to him, this recitation of scientific facts and complications. The words gave him an anchor of calmness, however precarious it might have been.

He told us about the pulsars, as he had already told me. He told us how the ship's systems could use the pulsars as a positioning reference, even if there was a problem with the NavNet.

"It should have been simple," he said, still shaking, still pale, but at least able to get a sentence out now. "There are bright pulsars and faint ones. We'd only have needed to lock onto a few bright ones to get a good enough fix—the Sphinx, the Monkey, a handful of others. But it still didn't work! The signals we were detecting were too far from the expected frequencies for the automatic correlators to work. That was my fault—I hadn't allowed for a wide enough temporal search window!"

"Meaning what?" Spry asked.

"All pulsars gradually slow down, as they lose

rotational energy. That's a known, a given. The pulse rate slowly decreases . . . but even after years and years, the frequency's only meant to change by tiny fractions of a millisecond." Prad swallowed hard. "Barely any change at all over a human lifetime. Yes, there are complicating factors—glitches which make pulsars spin faster or slower, very suddenly. That's why we need a few for our sample, to iron out those effects. I allowed for all that. But still—the correlators couldn't get a lock. I was searching out across decades of time. I told them to look a whole century ahead, just in case."

"A century?" Yesli asked, as if she might have misheard. "You think we might have been out here *that* long?"

"It's worse," I said. "Isn't it, Prad?"

Prad gave a dry, humourless laugh. "Oh, yes. It's quite a bit worse. Shall we say—by at least five hundred years?"

"No," Crowl said, in flat rejection of this possibility. "That's simply not possible. The ship's intact, apart from some power blackouts. We skipped, that's all, and something went a little wrong with one of the skips. But we haven't been out here for *five hundred years.*"

"You're right," Prad said, with an ominous smile. "Five hundred years is the lower end of my time estimate. This is the least worse case. You can be sure we've been lost quite a bit longer than that."

"Give me the worst case," I said.

"I cannot put a hard number on that—too many independent variables, too much uncertainty due to the glitches. It could be anything up to a thousand years, maybe a little more. Five thousand, if we have been very, very unlucky. There are some other things I can look at, if you really feel that your lives would be improved by knowing. Expansion patterns of visible supernova remnants. The proper motions of stars, now that we know which system we're in."

"And do we?" Yesli asked.

"I think so," Prad said. "In fact, it's exactly where we were meant to be. I'd say we were late arriving, but for all we know we've been in orbit here for centuries—just waiting for the ship to wake itself up."

"I don't understand," I said.

"You do, Scur—you just don't *want* to understand. This is Tottori, the heavily settled and industrialised world where we were supposed to be sent on for additional processing."

I remembered our earlier conversation. "You said you didn't recognise this place."

"I didn't."

"Well, then . . ." I started to say.

"There's been an ice age," Prad said. "That's why it

looks different. The icecaps are much larger, and the coastlines and surface features totally altered. Some of the seas have frozen, some have retreated. I don't know why this has happened."

"Ice ages happen," Spry said.

"The planet's tilt can't account for it. The sun is a little fainter than it should be, but not enough for this. I thought I must be wrong. Do you know why else I doubted myself?" He was staring at us now as if facing his accusers.

"It's all right, Prad," I said.

"There are no stations here. No orbital structures, habitats . . . no other ships. No cities, no spaceports, no roads or towns on the surface. This should be one of the most populous planets in human space . . . and instead it's just a shivering dead iceball."

After a lengthy silence Spry said: "Is it possible you've made a mistake?"

"It's possible," Prad answered, and we all allowed ourselves a foolish glimmer of hope, at least for the few seconds until Prad crushed it. "It's possible that my methods are faulty, yes. But when the data said that this was Tottori, do you think I just *stopped*, accepting it without question?"

"Go on," I said, with a horrible sense of inevitability.

"I checked the planet below against the ones in

the files. The other planets in the system, their orbits and sizes are all as they should be. There's a problem with the files, but . . ." Prad trailed off, collected himself. "I managed to recover enough information for the comparison. It's true that the coastlines look different now. Everything looks different. But there are still enough points of similarity to rule out any doubt. Believe me, I would much rather that planet was not Tottori. But it is."

— ✷ —

The Trinity—Yesli, Spry and Crowl—agreed to return to their respective wheels. They were going to have to do some delicate work in preparing the ground for the bad news we would all have to share sooner or later. They could not expect everyone to absorb the truth in a calm and reasonable manner.

For the most part, since the wakening, it had been soldiers against soldiers. Those old differences would not be buried by this latest development—far from it—but I could easily imagine the soldiers turning *en masse* against Prad and the other crew. After all, they were the ones responsible for the ship, and it was the ship that had dragged us across time.

Even if the fault lay with the ship, we needed it

to survive. There would also be no point in hanging the crew, even if it helped the soldiers deflect some of their energies. What they needed—what all of us needed—was another focus.

Fortunately I had just the man in mind.

From their individual wheels, Yesli, Spry and Crowl selected a dozen or so subordinates who could be trusted to organise the search for Orvin. They were trusted with weapons, broken out of the same store where Prad had acquired his gun. When there were not enough energy pistols to go around, they were given axes and heavy-duty wrenches from the tools store. They were also given slates—Prad had already located several dozen without searching particularly hard—and they were shown how to use the slates as communication devices, so that we could coordinate the search effort.

They were also, almost as an afterthought, informed that we appeared to be overdue at our destination by quite a long time.

Exactly how long?

Years, decades?

"More than a century," was the official line. It was not exactly the truth, but not exactly a lie either. No mention of the possibility of *thousands of years*.

Was it arrogant of us to think we could bear the truth, when the others could not? I do not think so. I had seen Prad nearly vomit from the shock of his discovery, and I was only just bearing it myself. And even then, I had reached no kind of emotional reckoning with the facts. I kept telling myself that not only would I not be returning home, but that there could not possibly be any home that I would ever recognise. My mother, my father, gone for thousands of years—every part of their lives lost, for all I knew, under another ice age, on another world.

I knew it, and believed it. But like a patient given an upsetting diagnosis, I was more shocked than accepting. That would come, given time, but for now all I felt was hollow, as if I had left some vital, living part of me in hibo.

If one thing helped me focus, it was the idea of finding Orvin. I do not mind admitting that I fantasized about what I would do to him. Sooner or later, in the absence of external authority, we would have to arrive at some sort of judicial apparatus aboard the *Caprice*—a system of laws and penalties, and a body of officials tasked with enforcing them. We would have to be careful of our actions, for fear of being held to account when we eventually recontacted whatever had become of human civilisation. We would not wish to have acted barbarically.

Until those laws were in place, though, we could allow ourselves a little latitude. Orvin, disliked even by many of his own side, would make an effective hate figure. I felt that that could be useful, when our own differences lay so close to the surface.

Mainly, though, I wanted him for myself.

I thought it most likely that Orvin would have tried to lose himself in Yesli's wheel, where he stood the least chance of being recognised by another soldier. In fact it was Crowl's party who found him.

I had warned the Trinity that Orvin was an extremely dangerous man, not merely a soldier but also an unsurpassed expert in armed and unarmed close quarters combat. I was not in any way convinced that Orvin was going to come quietly, just because we had him cornered. To that end, Yesli, Spry and Crowl had all agreed that their search parties would identify Orvin and proceed no further once his location was known. Once we had him pinned down, the other wheels would send over their own armed parties. Sooner or later we were going to have to mix, and this exercise would give the three different factions a chance to work together under a common goal.

That was the plan. It might have worked, if Crowl had not decided that his party could take Orvin without outside assistance. By the time we knew what was happening, the rest of us were still on our way to Crowl's wheel.

This, more or less, is what happened.

Orvin, who had surely been aware of the search parties closing in, allowed himself to be cornered. He appeared to give up without a fight, meekly accepting of his fate. Three of Crowl's people had him held down, while two more aimed guns at him. If I had been there I would have told them three was nowhere near enough. Maybe five or six might have made a difference.

Crowl's error was thinking it was safe to get in close, now that he had Orvin under restraint. Witness reports differ at this point, and since I wasn't present I shall not offer any definite account of events. But it seems that Orvin twisted free of his would-be captors, startling them with a sudden explosion of strength.

Rather than attempting to make a run for it—he could probably have shouldered his way through twenty or thirty people without difficulty—Orvin instead made a grab for Crowl. An instant later, he had some sort of weapon pressed against Crowl's throat. It was hard to see in his huge, baby-fingered hand. It was either a knife or an improvised blade of sharpened metal, depending on who you listened to.

Whatever it was, we never found it.

Orvin drew blood, but did not push the edge any deeper into Crowl's neck. He had made his point.

Crowl attempted to say something.

Orvin said: "Move aside. Those of you with weapons, throw them aside."

Orvin was behind Crowl now, one arm hooked around his chest and the other holding the edge against his throat.

Guns dropped to the floor.

"Kick those little toys out of reach."

Guns were kicked away.

"Scur?" Orvin said, raising his voice. "I heard you earlier, so I presume you can also hear this. I'm moving out of the wheel. You and everyone else will clear the elevator shaft and retreat to your own wheels. I expect to see no one in the central spine. Is that understood?"

We were about to begin the ascent to Crowl's wheel. Prad showed me how to make my voice heard.

"This won't work, Orvin. There's nowhere to go."

"It's a big ship, Scur. Why don't you let me be the judge of that?"

"Submit to our justice, Orvin. We'll treat you fairly."

"I heard your plans for me involved being tortured to death. Or was that just a rumour?"

I wondered who had allowed this to come to Orvin's attention.

"Just let Crowl go. He isn't part of this."

"He made himself part of it, Scur."

— ✕ —

In a sense, we owe Orvin a small debt of gratitude. If he had not acted the way he did, and not done what he did to Crowl, we would not have discovered the greater truth of our situation, the very reason that I am carving these words. Or, more properly, not as soon as we did. And since every day was soon to count, it was better to know sooner than later.

So, yes, we have that much to thank Orvin for.

— ✕ —

Acceding to his request—what choice did we honestly have—we allowed Orvin to make his way out of the wheel with Crowl as his hostage. Prad tracked the descent of the elevator all the way back to the central spine. In Yesli's wheel, Prad and I tried to find a camera angle that would allow us to pick up Orvin's subsequent progress. It was a hopeless task.

Parts of the ship were dark, depressurised or blind. In the other areas, all we saw were views of empty corridors and rooms.

Until, not more than an hour after Orvin had escaped the wheel, we found Crowl.

He was lolling against a wall in one of the near-weightless areas. Prad said Orvin must have moved into that sector since the last time he had made a check on that particular camera.

"That's blood," Yesli said, indicating a smear along part of the wall.

Crowl's form moved. He was pressing a blood-mittened hand to his stomach. His head turned slowly to look at the camera, his expression oddly placid.

I asked Prad if I could speak to him.

"Go ahead. The rest of the ship will hear, but I don't think that matters now."

"Crowl, this is Scur. We can see you, and we're on our way. Just hang in there."

As if anything I said was going to make a difference to his chances.

— ✖ —

I suppose I gave Orvin some thought as we made our way down to his victim, but I remember nothing of that now. What had happened to Crowl in no way altered Orvin's chances of evading us. Next time, I would make sure we were better prepared.

Crowl was still alive when we reached him. He had been stabbed, at least once, and there was quite some blood loss from the wound. He had done what he could to staunch the bleeding, but his efforts had only been partially successful. Besides, there was no telling the damage done under his skin.

But he was still conscious, still able to hear us.

"Listen to me," I said, while the others fussed around to find something that could double as a stretcher. "Prad says that there's a state of the art surgical suite aboard this ship, put there for the highest paying luxury tourists. He's warming it up right now. It'll be ready in minutes, but first we have to get you there, and secondly you have to hold out long enough for the auto-surgeon to wake up. Can you do that for me, Crowl?"

But Crowl was long past the point of being able to give me a coherent answer. Still, his eyes were open, which I took to be a sign that there was still some fight in him.

He was slipping away while we searched for a stretcher, so in the end we decided that the best course of action was to carry him with us, as gently as we could manage. It caused him pain, being moved like that, but if the pain kept him conscious I saw that as no bad thing. On the way to the elevator, and up to the surgical bay in the second wheel (surgery is much easier under gravity), Crowl made a medley of sucking, gurgling and whimpering noises. It was hard not to feel for him.

"We'll get the fucker," I said, trying to take his mind off the injury. "Even if we have to tear this ship apart."

Crowl moved his lips as if he wanted to say something in return, but it was too hard for him.

"You'll be all right," Spry said. "I know it hurts, but it's nothing the surgical suite won't be able to fix."

It was true: we had all seen worse injuries in combat, and many of us had survived them. But in the field you were seldom far from an anaesthetic patch or the tender ministrations of a medic.

As the elevator rose, Prad's voice came out of the walls. "I'm at the med bay. I hope you're not in a hurry."

"Of course we're in a fucking hurry!" I said. "What's wrong?"

"Place is dead and cold. No one's touched it since we woke."

"Then start waking it up!" Yesli shouted.

"I have," Prad said. "As soon as I opened the door, it kickstarted some of the automatic systems. Lights, heating and so on. But we may need a few minutes before the surgical systems come back to life."

I was about to say that Crowl's time might not be measurable in minutes.

"Speed it if up if you can, Prad. Does the gear look all right?"

"Yes—it's all still here and it all looks clean and undamaged. Not that I am any sort of an expert."

Behind Prad's voice I heard the sudden click, whirr and whine of waking machinery.

"What was that?"

"Some sort of check-out cycle," Prad said, sounding encouraged. "Lots of displays lighting up and things moving around all of a sudden."

"That sounds good. If you know how, start prepping the auto-surgeon to deal with an abdominal injury . . . stabbing . . . whatever you want to call it. Crowl's bleeding out pretty fast here. The sooner we can get to work, the better."

"I shall do what I can," Prad said.

Under his breath Spry said to me: "This could be an interesting test case, Scur. Sooner or later more of us are going to need medical attention of one kind or another. If we can't get that auto-surgeon to work, we could be in a lot of trouble."

"That's brightened my day."

"I'm just looking ahead. It's all very well surviving

the next few days or weeks. But if Tottori is as deserted as it looks, we're going to be in for a long wait."

"Maybe we can skip somewhere else, once the ship finishes waking up."

"Yes, and maybe it's the same story wherever we go. You heard Prad. The NavNet beacons aren't just silent in this system—there's nothing out there at all. I'm just saying we may have to rely on the resources at hand."

This did nothing to lift my mood, but by the time we reached the surgical bay I started feeling slightly better about Crowl's chances. The air in the room was still cold, but all the lights were on and the medical systems, to my untrained eye, looked ready to perform their chores. Prad stood next to an angled plinth, its upper surface flickering with anatomical diagrams.

Beyond the plinth was the glass-walled sterile enclosure of the auto-surgeon.

"Well?" I asked.

"I've done what I can. There is a problem with some of these routines . . . some kind of low-level corruption. I mentioned the problem with the ship's file system earlier? This is similar. I wish there were time to rebuild the command architecture."

"There isn't. Can we make do?"

"The surgeon may need some manual guidance."

I looked at Crowl, painted in blood. "For his sake, I hope it's nothing complicated."

"It shouldn't be. The machine will just prompt us for input when it must take a critical decision. Let's get him into the theatre."

Doors slid open in the side of the sterile enclosure. We positioned Crowl on the operating couch, leaving him in the blood-drenched clothes he had been wearing. Surrounding the couch were many articulated robotic surgical devices, ready to spring into swift and precise movement as soon as the sterile seal was re-established. Most of these devices ended in something sharp or dangerous. They reminded me of the hinged mouthparts of a flytrap.

I could not wait to leave Crowl alone, and be out of the enclosure.

The doors whisked tight. The air in the enclosure turned milky, then cleared—some kind of aggressive sterilisation procedure. Crowl was barely stirring now—he had been sinking into unconsciousness as we neared the bay.

"It should proceed automatically," Prad said, just as parts of the auto-surgeon began to swing into place. The machine clamped an anaesthetic mask over Crowl's face, then positioned a transcranial device over his skull. Meanwhile other parts of it moved to provide gentle restraint. I shuddered, remembering the way Orvin's soldiers had held me down in the bunker.

"We need to be realistic about his chances," Spry said in a low voice.

"You were the one who told him this was fixable."

"I was being upbeat."

"The surgeon must think it can finish the job," I said. But I had nothing to bolster this statement.

"It seems to be targeting the right area," Prad observed, as multiple operating arms concentrated their activities around the wound. "That's encouraging. The core routines can't be as scrambled as they looked."

"All it has to do is heal a knife wound," Yesli said. "We're not asking it to take out a brain tumour."

As if gaining confidence in its own abilities, the auto-surgeon's movements had quickened to an efficient blur, far too rapid for the human eye to track. I shuddered to think that there was a living form at the focus of that flickering silver storm. But the rational part of my mind told me that a machine was the only thing you wanted anywhere near an injured human being. Machines were ruthlessly infallible. In their mindless capacity for speed and precision they had saved far more lives than the kindliest, most well-intentioned of human doctors. But it was hard to keep this thought intact as the arms became a steely threshing engine.

"How deep do you think that wound went?" Spry asked.

"It must be hitting complications," I said.

But even I caught the edge of doubt in my own voice. Why was this demonically fast machine making such a meal of things?

Blood hit the glass. It was more than just a few drops, hurled away from the wound by the speed of the arms. This was a broad crimson banner, daubed in an instant. It was followed by a second, a wider, thicker swathe, and then a lumpy starburst, as if a blood grenade had just detonated.

"Fuck," I said.

"Shut it down!" Spry shouted.

Prad's hands moved on the plinth. "Trying."

So much blood had hit the glass that our view of Crowl was obstructed. I moved around to the right. I had, for an instant, a clear line of sight onto the spectacle. The auto-surgeon no longer seemed to be operating on Crowl. It was digging into him—digging *through* him, it looked, as if the machine was trying to treat some injury lodged not deep inside Crowl, but deep inside the couch on which he lay. The arms were scooping aside obstruction after obstruction, flinging these pieces away as if they were of no more interest than dirt or topsoil.

My view, as I said, lasted only an instant before the machine appeared to fling blood in my direction, spattering against the glass. Now there was a solid, ropy mass contained within the spatter.

"Make it stop!" Spry shouted, as if, by this point, it was going to make much difference to Crowl.

But Prad could not make the auto-surgeon stop. He jerked back from the plinth, studying the tips of his fingers as if he had been stung. "It's no good," he said. "I can't even open the sterile doors."

The machine, by now, had turned the inside of the operating theatre into a cylinder of red, its perfection marred only by the hints of anatomy glued to the glass.

"Someone give me an axe," I said.

One of Yesli's people had an axe. They passed it to Yesli and Yesli, after a moment's hesitation, passed it to me. It was bright red and had obviously never been used. I went to the door and swung the axe with its blunt edge to the glass doors, over and over, until finally the doors shattered into a million pink-stained shards.

I crunched through them, squinting against the blood haze filling the air. The noise of the auto-surgeon was a constant metallic scissoring, like knives being sharpened and sharpened. I was aware, distantly, that an automated voice had begun to warn of the breech of the sterile field.

As if it mattered to any of us.

"Can you make it stop?" I shouted back to Prad.

"I don't know! I think something . . ."

I could see very little of the botched operation. Crowl was a bloodied mass, but then again so was the auto-surgeon. It had lavished every part of itself in gore. Yet it seemed also to be slowing, the movement of its parts becoming easier to track. Either it was coming to the natural end of its maniacal procedure or my arrival had interrupted it. Crowl had to be dead, I told myself. There was no point in wasting a single bullet on him to make sure of that fact.

I swung the axe again, but this time bringing down the blade. I aimed it at the approximate area of Crowl's head.

And by then the auto-surgeon was still.

"Sterile field is breeched," the voice was still saying. "Optimum hygienic integrity may have been compromised."

— ✖ —

In the difficult days following the death of Crowl we came to a better understanding of our predicament.

We gathered in one of the main cargo bays to hear Prad's findings. There was no gravity in the bay—it was near the middle of the ship, not in one of the wheels—so we had positioned ourselves at all angles, hooked off the walls or the many bulky items of cargo, while Prad floated with his legs tucked under him. He made me think of a frog on an invisible lily pad.

"On a practical level," he began, "I am pleased to report that there is no reason not to trust the auto-surgeon."

This was met with a chorus of black laughter and swearing.

"The machine did not set out to kill Crowl," Prad persisted. "Its programming was damaged."

"That's an understatement," Spry murmured, not far to my left. Then, in a more constructive tone: "It seemed to be trying to rip him apart. How are any of us expected to trust that thing now?"

"I have rebuilt the architecture. It had not assembled properly, when we tried using the surgery bay so quickly after revival. Some earlier instruction fragments were still lodged in its memory. The machine became . . . confused. Schizophrenic. It was trying to do its best."

More black laughter.

"That doesn't really answer my question," Spry said. He was next to Yesli, and next to Yesli was Sacer, the replacement for Crowl. Sacer was another woman, a command-level officer about ten years older than me.

The floating Prad gave a pragmatic shrug. "The choice will always be ours, whether or not we place our faith in the auto-surgeon. It is the only such facility we have. In a matter of dire medical emergency, what other choice would we have?"

"Would you put yourself in that thing?" I asked.

"Of course. It's just a machine. It was broken before, so it did not work properly. Now I have made it better. The auto-surgeon, at least. The sterile field is still broken, and we do not have the means to repair that. We will need to be very careful about infection, when next we operate. Although I fear that infection will, over the course of time, prove to be the least of our worries."

"Meaning what?" Sacer asked.

"I had hoped that the auto-surgeon's damaged architecture would be an isolated problem." Some air current was making Prad tilt head over heels, very slowly, like a tumbling asteroid. "It is not. The malaise is much more widespread. Every system in this ship that depends on an instruction set or a database is affected, to one degree or another. Records and files are widely unreadable. The ship has been moving information around inside itself, trying to preserve the most vital parts—those that it needs to keep basic operational systems running. In the process, it has had to make certain sacrifices."

"Explain," I said.

"If I may simplify . . ."

"Please do."

"The ship has two types of memory. Like the human brain, it has both long- and short-term storage registers. The long-term registers are normally very stable, but slower to access and update. Into these areas the ship would normally consign information that does not need to be consulted or updated very frequently."

"Such as?" Spry asked.

"Historical data. Cultural knowledge. Maps of planetary surfaces. Astrogation files. Medical data— how to operate on a patient. That sort of thing."

"And now?" I pushed.

"There is a fault with the volatile memory, the kind that the ship uses for short-term, immediate recall—its working memory, so to speak. As a result, the ship has been forced to commandeer portions of its long-term memory for routine functions that would normally only ever trouble the volatile part—

basic housekeeping, really. It has been doing its best not to overwrite critical data, but since it has been in this difficult condition for rather a long time . . ."

"How bad is it?" Sacer asked.

The upside down Prad swallowed. "My investigations have only been preliminary. But already I have found huge areas of memory scrambled beyond recall. I was lucky with the auto-surgeon's architecture—I think it is repaired—but in many instances there is no backup, no recoverable copy. The data that is gone, is *gone*. Worse, the process is continuing. Now that we are awake, the demands on the ship have only increased. The rate of data attrition has definitely quickened. The ship is forgetting itself more rapidly than before."

"Wait," Spry said slowly. "This isn't fatal, is it? The data that's being lost . . . scrambled . . . whatever? It's not vital to the ship?"

"Not vital to the ship, but possibly vital to us," said Yesli.

"On a basic level," Prad said, "the ship can still keep functioning for quite some time. There are questions of supplies, of fuel, of closed-cycle systems that are not working as efficiently as they should, of things for which we do not have spare parts. But if all else fails, we can all of us return to hibo and instruct the ship to return to a powered-down configuration.

Long before that happens, though, large swathes of the memory will have been lost forever. At the present rate, we are losing about one-third of one percent of the total stored memory for every day that we are awake."

"That doesn't sound too bad," I said.

"On a day to day basis," Prad answered, "we'd hardly notice the difference. The sectors are being over-written in a random fashion, depending only on the ship's immediate requirements. But in a thousand days, give or take, we will have lost *everything*. Every single piece of information not absolutely vital to the continued functioning of the ship will have been overwritten. Our history. Our art. Our science and medicine. Our music. Images of your homeworlds—people we knew and loved. Anything that isn't in our heads, it's gone for good. A great deal has already been lost."

"Then we'll just have to manage without it," I said, with an icy resolve that surprised even me. "It's a luxury, that's all. What matters is keeping alive, keeping the ship functioning. The universe hasn't ended. The information's all still out there somewhere."

"We hope," Prad answered.

"What about the skip systems?" Spry asked. "If we need help, we need to get somewhere where we'll have a chance of finding it. Another system, where they can patch us up."

"To attempt a skip without NavNet referencing would be very unusual," Prad said.

"If it's a choice between that and dying here, I'll take that chance," Yesli replied.

"I will need to look carefully at the condition of the hypercore," Prad said. "There may have been damage. There may be damage that we cannot even detect until the moment of skip."

"And then what?" Sacer asked.

"It would be quick and painless," Prad answered.

— ✖ —

It was never a question of our not finding Orvin.

The ship was big, but it was not infinite. There were many of us and only one of him. He had gone into hiding with only a makeshift weapon and the clothes on his back. He had no ready access to food or water, and if he had need of medicine (it was hard to say if he had been injured or not) he had no access to that either. If he tried to escape down to the planet's surface, he would need to get past the armed teams we stationed at the lifeboats and pods.

We had no reason to assume that Orvin had any

better knowledge of the ship's secrets than the rest of us. What he did have was guile, ruthlessness and determination. On the other hand, we had force of numbers and the slates.

The slates became our salvation, although we did not know that at the time. We had located about a hundred that were still in a functioning order, along with many more that were dead or in some way damaged. They were not complicated devices and there was a limit to what could be done with them, even when they were working properly. But they were also sturdy and easy to use, even for grunts like me. Prad and the other crew took turns instructing the rest of us how to display a visualisation of the ship's layout, a schematic that could be as detailed or as simple as we needed.

They had their limitations, too. I had thought, cleverly, that we might be able to solve the memory leak by copying everything onto the slates, but Prad had already ruled out that option. The slates could search and display any information held in the ship's memory, but they had no long-term storage capacity of their own.

"They are windows, that's all," Prad explained sadly. "They can display, but they cannot *retain*."

For now, in our search for Orvin, windows were all that we required. It was not that we had any pressing need to find him. There was a limit to the harm he could do, hidden away in the shadows. But the thought of him being at large was intolerable. More than anything, as the fear spread, we needed the focus that Orvin provided.

My dreams in this period were almost always nightmares. I took to sleeping in a hibo capsule, the way many of us did. I snuggled into a nest of prison clothing and tried not to think of better times.

— ✳ —

Prad was the first to notice the anomaly. He had been working hard to bring as many of the ship's cameras back into action. This would help with the search effort, but it would also enable us to get a better impression of *Caprice's* overall spaceworthiness. If there was something wrong with the outside of the ship—some damage that was not registering on the internal displays—Prad felt we ought to know about it sooner rather than later.

We found damage and plenty of it, although nothing as serious as we might have feared. The hull had suffered a constant bombardment of micro-meteorite strikes and cosmic ray impacts, leaving it peppered with craters and burns. Markings and lettering had been scoured away to bare plating, and the plating in turn had been pricked and hammered like worn-out battle armour. It looked terrible, but Prad assured me that there was very little that was of immediate concern. As scarred as the ship now was, it had been engineered to take much worse.

"We can fix the problem areas," he said, with a breezy confidence that I did not quite share. "Go out in suits, with basic repair equipment. That is not a priority, at least for the moment." And now Prad jabbed his thumb at a part of the ship captured by one of the external cameras. "*This* is."

"You're going to have to help me out. One lumpy mechanical thing looks much like another lumpy mechanical thing."

"It is a vehicle," Prad answered. "It is not one of ours. And it was mostly definitely not docked with *Caprice* when we prepared for our last skip."

"You can be sure of that?"

"Nothing would have been allowed to remain docked—it upsets the skip equilibrium. But I would have remembered in any case. That is a very odd looking ship. If I did not know better, I would say it belongs in a museum."

"If it wasn't docked with us when we skipped . . . then how did it get here?"

"If I might be permitted to venture a theory . . ."

But Prad was going to venture his theory whether I wanted it or not. "From here, there does not seem to be very much to that ship. Just a capsule, with some steering and docking capability. I do not believe it could have travelled very far."

"Then it's come up from Tottori?"

"One imagines. I should like to get a closer look at it, to get a better idea of how long it has been docked."

I squinted through sleep-deprived eyes at the image Prad was showing me. It was still just a lump to my eyes, a grey thing barnacled to a bigger, more complicated grey thing. I could barely see where one ship began and the other ended.

But I trusted Prad.

"You're right, we have to get to it. But I have no idea what part of the ship you're showing me."

Prad snatched one of the functioning slates and produced a schematic. "This is where it is docked—forward six. That's a whole section we've yet to enter. There is certainly no power there, and there may or may not be air."

"Based on what we know, could Orvin have made it into that area?"

"I think it doubtful. In any event, there are other lifeboats that would be closer to him, if escape was his intention. We have protected those that we can reach, and I have tried to disable all escape systems from central control. That is not infallible, of course—you are not *supposed* to be able to disable them in that manner, and there are loopholes that a resourceful man could find, given . . ." A sudden focus returned to him. "What I am saying is, we have done what we can. More than likely Orvin can't reach this thing—and he certainly won't know of its existence while he remains in hiding. But at any cost, we must reach it."

"I agree. Even if we have to step down the number of search parties, it's worth the delay in capturing Orvin. You think we'll find answers, don't you?"

"I am certain of it," Prad said. "Whether they are the answers we will care for, that is something else entirely. Anyway, *I* do not care to have something attached to my ship."

"Our ship," I corrected under my breath.

— ✳ —

Three of us went: Prad, Yesli and I.

Under other circumstances, it would have taken only a few minutes to reach the docking bay where the mysterious object had clamped on. In fact it took nearly ten hours, trying one route and then another, hoping that we would not open a door and find vacuum beyond it, and not always being able to say for certain until Prad forced the door to operate. Where the ship was pressurised, it was often unbearably cold. Even if air did lie beyond a particular bulkhead or lock, it was not always possible to find our way through into that section. Some doors simply would not open, no matter the persuasion Prad brought to the matter. Others, when they were finally made to work, showed signs of vandalism or force applied to the other side. One entire section of the ship between us and the capsule, remained depressurised, so rather than make a time-consuming detour we broke a set of spacesuits out of storage and used them instead. It was my first time in vacuum gear and I found the experience bruising and uncomfortable, although no worse in its way than combat armour. Prad was philosophical. The more of us that had some experience of suits, the quicker we could fix the areas of the hull that needed attention. It was a bigger job than the crew could fix on their own, and we would all need to work together to get it done.

Work together, I thought? Dregs like us?

But I did not want Prad to know how hopeless I thought that was. If he still had faith in human nature, I would not be the one to prick his bubble.

From a window near the lock, Prad was able to

get a better look at our foreign visitor. He studied it wordlessly for at least a minute.

"Well?" Yesli asked.

"It's as I thought," he said. "A simple capsule, with a docking attachment. You see how complicated it is?"

"I'll take your word for it."

"The capsule is stone age. But the docking attachment is really quite sophisticated. See all those moving parts? I think there is a reason for that. Whoever came up here did not know quite what to expect when they arrived. They couldn't have been sure what design of lock they would have to allow for!" Prad was smiling despite himself, in pure academic delight at an engineering conundrum. "That docking attachment of theirs is a sort of universal key, able to fit around almost any configuration of lock. Within reason. That tells you something, doesn't it? We have been using a standard lock for centuries! How could anyone have forgotten that?"

"Not easily," I said.

"I'll offer another observation. That capsule must have been brought here by another ship—a booster rocket, perhaps, to lift it from Tottori. I doubt that they had much weight to spare, and yet they went to all that trouble to provide a universal docking system. That meant they were very, very keen to get aboard our ship."

"They succeeded," Yesli said.

"Their idea of success," Prad said, "may have involved going home as well. In that respect they do not seem to have been quite as fortunate."

"So someone knew we were here, and tried to get aboard," I mused. "But they know so little about us they couldn't even be sure what type of lock we use."

In hindsight we were in far too much haste to look inside the capsule, given that it could have contained anything from a booby-trap to contagion. We were lucky: when we opened the lock, and climbed into the little vehicle (it was large enough for only one of us at a time) there was nothing inside to harm us. The capsule held a sort of couch, which seemed designed to force a person into the least comfortable posture imaginable, and packed around this couch, in addition to padding and restraints, was an assortment of primitive controls. It was all clean and new, but that meant nothing given how long our own ship had been powered down and cold.

Prad examined it all methodically.

"What are you looking for?" I asked, as he fingered his way around cables and straps and metal boxes.

"Something with a memory," he answered. "Something we might be able to use."

But there was nothing that would have made the slightest difference to our own plight. The capsule had some electrical storage cells which had now run out of power, and these in turn would have operated mechanical navigation equipment and life-support devices. But there was nothing that could store an image, or hold so much as a page of text.

There was also no sign of an occupant.

But someone had flown this thing here—it could not possibly have docked on its own, given the simplicity of its automatic systems. They had docked, opened our airlock, entered our ship.

And then not left.

"Now there are two of them," Yesli said. "One man we would like to catch. And someone else we didn't know was aboard. Our problem has become twice as difficult."

"There'll be a body somewhere," I said. "That's what we look for. The body of whoever brought this thing here. They came, found a dead ship, couldn't leave again."

"You don't think the newcomer could still be alive?" Prad asked.

"Do you see any sign that Tottori could have launched this thing recently? A city, an industrial capacity?"

"We haven't really been looking that hard," Yesli pointed out.

"Not too hard to miss a fucking spaceport, a rocket

pad. Much more likely that this thing came up years ago, before the ice closed in. Centuries, maybe."

"Then yes, we are probably looking at a body," Yesli said.

"Or not," Prad added.

"I don't follow."

"There are hibo caskets, Scur. Whoever flew this thing would not have been a fool. Maybe they couldn't leave, for whatever reason. But they might have been able to make it to the caskets. Find one that was empty, or open one that was already occupied. Take the place of whoever was inside it."

"Murder, you mean?" Yesli asked.

"Supposition," Prad said. "I am just saying that there are possibilities we should not discount. One of us—I mean, one of the survivors—crew or . . . otherwise. One of us *could be* from the planet below." He paused. "Except not the crew, obviously. There aren't many of us left, and we all know each other. But would you soldiers or civilians know if one of you didn't belong?"

"None of us fucking *belong*," I clarified.

"I mean in the sense that there is someone who was not even from the war. Not even from our own time. Would you necessarily know? You are all strangers now."

"We would need to know," Yesli said. "For the

safety of the ship. For the knowledge they might have. We would need to find this stowaway, if they aren't already dead. For the moment, that is more important than finding a war criminal."

"Well, you can rule me out," I said. "Orvin knew me, and I knew Orvin. That eliminates both of us."

"I would not have ranked you very high in the list of suspects," Yesli said.

"It wouldn't have mattered whether you knew Orvin or not," Prad said. "You are a soldier. From our conversations, it is clear that you believe that you have a slow bullet inside you. I have no reason to doubt you."

"You can read the bullets," I said.

"Read the information in them, yes. The biographical military data, the medical histories. Even if I can't access any of that, the mere existence of a bullet will be enough to vindicate anyone's story. The stowaway almost certainly won't have one."

"Neither will any of the civilians," Yesli said.

"That is true, but the military prisoners constitute by far the biggest sample of our population. We can scan their bullets very easily—display the contents on a slate, if need be. It will be much easier than our original hunt for Orvin."

"And if all of us soldiers turn out to have bullets?"

"Then we move onto the civilians. They are smaller

in number and more inclined to stick together. Soldiers are habitually suspicious of their fellows—especially military prisoners."

"You're an expert now."

"I am merely making an observation, Scur. Civilians are garrulous. This is in their nature, especially when confronted with an unfamiliar situation. I imagine a stowaway would find it quite difficult to hide themselves effectively." He shrugged. "Whatever the case, we will find them sooner or later."

Yesli arranged another work team to search the capsule, and soon after that they found a spacesuit of unfamiliar design, stuffed into a locker not far from the docking port. In the meantime, Prad and I returned to the main part of the ship and prepared to coordinate the reading of the slow bullets.

"This is a distraction," I said. "I want Orvin, not this nameless stowaway."

"There's no law that says we can't look for two things at once." Prad was fiddling with his slate, adjusting the settings so that it could talk to my bullet. "Are you serious about Orvin—your intentions with him? Wouldn't it be enough to hand him over to the Trinity, let justice have its way?"

"He doesn't deserve justice."

"You frighten me a little, Scur. I wonder what you'd do to me, if I ever got on the wrong side of you."

"I'd think of something creative."

Prad handed me the slate as the information scrolled across its surface. "There. Solid read. A few corrupted sectors, some anomalous parity checks, but otherwise it's all still there."

I glanced at him. "Don't you want to read it yourself?"

"To check on your story?"

"You only have my word that I'm here because of some mistake. Maybe I lied about that. Maybe I'm as bad as all the rest of them—the worst of the worst. Maybe you *should* be afraid of me."

"And I'm a civilian technician. I wouldn't know one military history from another. Does it make some sort of sense to you? I want to make sure we're reading out your bullet, and not one belonging to someone in the next room."

"No," I said after a moment. "This is me." And I tilted the slate around for Prad's benefit. "These pictures—these are my mother and father." Blank faces, staring into government cameras on census day. "They were good people—too good for those around them. My father made enemies, by being a good man. They got at him by getting at me— arranging my conscription, even though I wasn't supposed to be put into the military." I stroked a finger across their images, wishing that they looked happier. "He blamed himself for it. They both blamed themselves. And when I was injured after the ceasefire, and put on this ship . . . they'd never have known what happened to me, would they?"

"We must all have been presumed lost," Prad offered.

"I wanted them to know I was all right, and that I didn't blame either of them. It wasn't their fault. And I wanted them to know that I'd made it through the war, that I was on my way home."

"I am sorry."

"You must have your own family, Prad."

"I do. Did. But there's no slow bullet inside me. No history, no images to recall."

"Then it's worse for you."

"I do not think it is easy for any of us. But I am glad that you have been validated. I did not doubt you, Scur."

"But others might have."

I scrolled down through the long accounting of my service history. It was all in here. Training, deployments—victories and losses. My injuries and recuperation episodes. Redeployment. Names and places I had already begun to forget.

"The bullets are safe, I suppose. If they've held the information this long, they must be immune to whatever's got hold of the ship." I held the slate against my chest, like a shield. "This is safe—it's always going to be there, inside me."

"I hope it gives you some strength, Scur."

"It will."

"But there will be difficulties ahead, I think. To an extent, our pasts are private now. They have been erased by the accident—the thing that happened to *Caprice*. But the bullets leave nothing to doubt. The worst of us will be known to us all."

"We'll have to deal with it. Openness, transparency."

Prad nodded. "But rather easy to say, when you have objective proof of your own innocence. Would you have been so eager to allow me to read the bullet, if you knew it revealed some awful crime you'd committed? Some terrible atrocity or moral failing? That you were a war criminal, a butcher, a defector or traitor?"

He was right, but I had no good answer for him.

— ✖ —

We do not choose our friends in life; life does that for us. Prad and I had nothing in common beyond our intertwined fates on *Caprice*. We had known different lives before the war and different lives during it. He had never been asked to kill someone, or hate someone for wearing a different uniform or believing in the words of a different Book. That was a difference which nothing could bridge.

But he was the first person I had spoken to since my awakening, and we had worked together to achieve that first flimsy truce. That was enough to force a bond between us. I felt I had more in common with Prad than with many of my fellow soldiers. Regardless of what side they had been on during the war, they had all done something to merit being on this ship—violated some rule or other. Some of those infractions might be minor or excusable—some might even, under the circumstances of combat, be morally justifiable.

But the point was that none of us could be sure. We were free to invent our pasts, to lie about what we had done or perhaps failed to do. On the contrary, though, I could be perfectly sure of myself. And I could be sure that Prad was just a technician, as innocent in his way as me. It meant that I found it easier to trust this man than any other soldier or civilian aboard the ship, save for the other crew. And I think Prad, being naturally fearful of the soldiers who made up the bulk of the awakened, was glad to have me as a reference point, a reassurance that warriors such as I did not automatically hold people like him in contempt.

"We can work together," I told him, when his doubts were surfacing. "It'll be hard, but we have no other choice. Fundamentally, we're all just human beings, caught up in some shit we didn't ask for."

"I have heard that soldiers are different," Prad said hesitantly. "Different from engineers and technicians like me, at any rate." There was a sort of diffidence in his voice, as if I might take offence at this generalisation.

"In what sense?"

"You soldiers tend to be believers. Many of you read the Book, one version of it or another. Is this not the case?"

"And it isn't like that with you and your colleagues?"

"Most of us, no," Prad said emphatically. "Of course I have known some technicians who were religiously inclined. But even then I never sensed that they took the writings all that seriously. It was more that they came from a family of believers, and they did not want to disappoint their elders or give up a custom too readily." After a moment he said: "Some of these people were even my friends. It was never against the law to have religious leanings, even in the technical staff of a Hundred Worlds starliner."

"Well, it's not too different for soldiers. Yes, many of us do read the Book—our version of it or theirs."

"The differences seem slight to outsiders."

"If you decide that these things matter at all, then so do the differences."

"And you, Scur—someone who took the differences seriously?"

I allowed a silence before answering—I did not want Prad to think that any of this was simple or beneath consideration.

"My parents both read the Book," I said. "They were believers, if you want to call them that. But it was not the only thing in their lives. My mother taught me Giresun's poetry—that was against the law. My father was also very open minded. He liked to mention that many of their prophets were our prophets, and vice versa. That many of the commandments were alike, word for word. Besides, it was never clear-cut: some of our side were allowed to read their Book, and some of their side were allowed to read *our* Book. Nothing is as simple as some people make out."

"But if your parents were believers, did you not follow their example?" Prad was squinting now, as if trying to follow a difficult calculation.

I shook my head. "I was schooled in the Book, made to memorise whole parts of it. So were we all. In that sense, the Book is part of me. I feel an affection for the language that I can't even begin to explain to you."

Prad nodded for me to continue.

"There's also a lot of common sense in it," I went on. "Just basic good advice for living a decent life, being kind, thinking of your neighbours and so on. My father was a devout man, but also honest in his business dealings. He took that from the Book, even though it brought trouble on us as a family."

"Then the Book can damage, if you follow it too literally."

"Perhaps. But there are also many parts that can help you when you have a difficult decision or are facing an unpleasant time in your life."

"But you do not, at heart, believe in its literal truth."

"If I ever did, I don't remember when I stopped believing. But that doesn't mean that I disowned the Book. The language was still as beautiful as ever, the wisdom just as comforting. When Orvin caught me, he thought he would hurt me by hurting my Book."

"Did he?"

"Less than he hoped for, but yes. I still did not like to see him doing what he did."

"This seems like a very enlightened attitude," Prad said. "I sincerely hope that it is shared by many of your fellows. If it is, there may yet be a chance we may be able to rub along."

"There will always be true believers."

"None of you came with your Books," Prad said.

"You had no possessions, nothing with you except the clothes you were wearing when you went into hibo. And there are no physical copies of the Book anywhere on this ship. Trust me: I would have seen them. What will the believers do now, without their scripture?"

"Learn to live without the Book," I said. "Just as we'll have to learn to live without many other things." Easier said than done, of course. But then I thought to add: "The ship's memory."

"What of it?"

"You said it contained cultural knowledge."

"This is true."

"You wouldn't have to believe in the Book, either theirs or ours, to regard the texts as having cultural value. They must still be in the memory, mustn't they?"

"They aren't," Prad said quickly. "I am afraid they were among the first sectors to be lost, when the ship had to protect its core data."

"You're sure of this?"

"Oh yes. It was one of the first things I checked. I am very sorry, Scur."

It never occurred to me to think that that was a very odd coincidence, that the Books should be lost so early in the great forgetting. But then I have always been a touch naïve.

— ✸ —

Just as no military plan ever survives the first contact with the enemy, so our search scheme proved hopelessly idealised.

We thought we had struck lucky early in the operation, when one of the soldiers appeared not to have a bullet. It was a woman who spoke in a dialect similar to my own, and who appeared to have no difficulty mixing with her fellow survivors. She had offered a convincing account of her wartime deeds. When she was brought before the Trinity she seemed properly fearful, unable to grasp why she had been singled out in this manner. Perhaps our newcomer was more skilled at blending in than I had presumed.

But Prad was wisely cautious. Yesli also noted that she was also too tall to have been a comfortable fit for the abandoned spacesuit.

"I have a bullet," the woman said, with fierce conviction. "I remember them putting it in. No one forgets that."

As it happened, there were others like her. It turned out that about one in twenty of us had bullets which were no longer working properly, no longer able to be addressed by the slates. Once we knew that it was easy enough to set up a second level of screening, using a portable medical scanner. But that was more time-consuming than the slates and it couldn't discriminate between a dead bullet and a piece of shrapnel that had a similar size and shape. More questioning was needed, and so the Trinity appointed additional interrogators to dig deeper into the accounts offered by these questionable cases.

One by one, all of them proved plausible.

We continued the search. There was unrest, but that was to be expected. People were already jumpy after Orvin's escape and the unpleasant business with Crowl. But we could not very well announce that there was likely to be an impostor among us. They would have torn apart anyone with a slightly odd dialect, a story with a few discrepancies.

In a sea of doubts you cling to the smallest of truths. I had Prad read out my bullet again. There was much more information in it than I could absorb on a single reading. It was touching, in a way, how much my superiors had felt they needed to know about me. It was all there, scrolling across the slate. Things I barely remembered about myself. You could reconstruct half my life from the bullet's whisperings.

But again and again, it was the pictures of my mother and father that I kept returning to. Gone now, of course. How could it be otherwise? They were as lost to me as I was to them. I wished that I had pictures of them as they were when they were happy, before politics and war and spitefulness made a mess of our lives.

But this was better than nothing.

— ✹ —

"I don't know what to do," Yesli said. "Whether to punish them, or reward them for their initiative."

"Punish them for what?" I asked.

"Vandalism."

With two search efforts ongoing—one to find Orvin, another to find our stowaway—it was amazing that our people had time for anything but sleep. But in fact they had time for a great many things, including fighting and fucking and telling stories.

Storytelling is another word for being interrogated.

To begin with it was a way of filling the dead hours, a way of not thinking about what was ahead of us. We all wanted to know who we had to share this ship with. But as news got out—as it was bound to do—that there was someone here who did not belong—the storytelling took on a different aspect. Now it had become a form of testing. The weak among us, those who had been born with a face that just happened to look suspicious, those who had something *else* to hide—these were the ones who were made to go over their stories again and again, in the hope that the telling would expose some latent falsehood. It was no different in kind to the interrogations being served out by the Trinity, but at least the Trinity was trying to be methodical and dispassionate. Some of these storytelling sessions did not go well for the teller. There were no deaths, yet, but there was blood and I knew we could not afford to fall back into chaos.

So when Yesli showed me the vandalism, I was actually pleased to see something that did not involve mutual fear and suspicion.

Using their slates, some of the search parties had begun to dig into the ship's slowly vanishing cultural memory. They knew that we had about a thousand days before all this knowledge would be lost, and this awareness had motivated them to preserve what they could.

The slates, as Prad had explained, had no memory of their own. But they could selectively display any record from the ship's total surviving memory. If this knowledge could be transcribed onto a different medium, it might yet be conserved. Clearly, we would have used paper if we had paper, and a means to mark it.

But we had walls, and ceilings, and floors. More walls and ceilings and floors than we could bare to imagine.

We had nothing that could mark a surface in the same manner as ink, but many tools that could scratch a line. So they took their slates, called up a record from memory, and engraved it into metal with sweat and muscle. By the time Yesli found out what they were doing, they had already covered several metres of corridor in lines both neat and less than neat. You could tell the hand of each scriber, and within each hand you could see the evidence of early clumsiness and slowly gathering ability. The first marks were scratchy, rife with mistakes. The letters and words were too large. As they progressed, a sort of confident regularity began to win through. They began to scratch in fine guiding lines, and set neat ordered words down on those staves.

It was easy to be selective, in those early days. Most people were keen to preserve some record that was of personal significance. A memory of their homeworlds, or even the region or city that they had held most dear. They could not go into any sort of detail, but this was a start, a tangible blow against the ship's own forgetting. There were songs and poems that held some particular fondness. Someone had even begun to record lines of musical notation, a fragment of some larger tune. It might as well have been random scratchings, for all the sense it made to me.

Later, I told Yesli that I did not think these people merited punishment.

"They haven't done any real damage. More than that, though. This is actually something useful. You've heard Prad talking about the memory loss. Unless we meet another ship, we're not going to be able to fix that in a thousand days. Now at least we have a means of preserving something."

Yesli could not help but laugh.

"Have you any idea of the amount of information Prad was talking about? It's beyond anything you or I are ever capable of imagining, let alone carving onto a wall inside a thousand days. This is . . . a gesture. Nothing more. A pointless, time-consuming gesture. It won't achieve anything."

"It'll make them feel like they can do something. And it doesn't have to be pointless. I know we can't record *everything*. I never said we could. But if these people had some guidance, some idea of the most vital things . . ."

"You're talking about scratching the most important parts of human cultural knowledge onto metal walls." Yesli allowed herself a silence. "In a thousand days."

"There are hundreds of us. Yes, we've a couple of fugitives to find right now. But they won't get away from us for long, and then what? If the people on this ship don't have something to do, something to keep hands and eyes occupied, there's going to be a bloodbath."

"Fine." Yesli had her arms folded. "So where would you propose we started?"

"That's not for me. You're the Trinity. Assign some experts to make the choices. How about basic medicine? We all saw what that machine did to Crowl. How are we going to cope when the machine doesn't even work? It would be good to have a few pointers—how to set a compound fracture, that sort of thing."

"Basic medicine, then. You think a wall will be enough?"

"I did say basic."

"I'm just trying to draw your attention to the logistical difficulties, Scur."

"I'm not blind to them. I'm just saying: What else do we do? Maybe we can only save a thousandth part of the memory this way. But it's the difference between saving a thousandth part and none at all. And maybe that thousandth part is the one thing that's going to save us, when things start getting really tough."

"I'd say a thousandth part is optimistic, Scur."

"Then I'm an optimist."

After a moment Yesli said: "If we did this, it would have to be on a fair and equal basis."

"Of course."

"Crew, civilians . . . soldiers. Everyone. Including the Trinity. There could be no favouritism."

"I wouldn't dream of it."

"The markings we've already seen . . . those people were doing it for their own satisfaction. No one was holding them to a schedule, forcing them to complete a passage within a certain time."

"It will need to be different," I agreed.

"Assigned work teams, just the way it is now. But each with a passage, a piece of knowledge, that must be committed to the wall. Laid down, in its entirety. We can't tolerate mistakes, not if there's going to be a point to this. If we want to save anything useful, enough to make it more than just a gesture . . . then it's going to be hard work. A massive collected effort. Something close to slave labour, except we'll all be slaves as well as masters. For a thousand days, all we'll live and breathe will be these metal walls. Until they crawl into our dreams. Until our fingers are bloodied stumps and the effort has driven us to the brink of madness."

"You might be in danger of talking me out of my own idea, Yesli."

"I just think we need a ready appreciation of what this will cost us. But you are perfectly right, Scur, all the same. Even if we only save a millionth or a billionth part of the total memory, that is still . . ." She hesitated.

"A light in the darkness?"

"Yes."

"Then we become that light," I said. "Even if it drives us mad. Even if it kills us."

— ✖ —

We found our stowaway on the fourth day of searching. It had only ever been a matter of time, a matter of methodical procedure, but it still felt like a victory. We needed something like that, in those early days, especially as we had yet to find Orvin. It bothered me that he was still out there. It was like sharing a room with a rat. I wanted the rat under my heel, so that I could crush it and sleep peacefully.

But at least we had found one hideaway.

Our stowaway was no one that I had suspected; no one that had caught my eye in the days since the wakening. That was because she had been doing the only sensible thing, which was to make herself as unobtrusive as possible. She had avoided all but the shallowest of exchanges with her fellow survivors. But once we started reading out the slow bullets, it was only a matter of time before she came to our attention.

When we knew who she was, we took her to the same control room where Prad and I had threatened to blow up the ship.

"Tell us your name," Yesli said.

"Murash."

She was very small, and looked even smaller jammed into a chair for questioning. I realised then that we should always have been looking for someone small, due to the size of the capsule. We could have spared ourselves days of searching.

"Do you know how we found you?" I asked.

"There are things inside you." She spoke in an odd but not too-odd dialect. "This is what you have been looking for."

"Things inside *some* of us," I told her, when it was just me, the Trinity and our prize, in one of the secure control rooms. "They're called slow bullets. Implants. You understand about implants?"

She gave me a withering look. She had a worn out, defeated look, with dark patches under her eyes. But then so did many of us.

"Yes, I understand."

"But you don't have anything like that yourself," Yesli said.

"No."

"How long have you been on our ship, Murash?" Spry asked.

"I do not know."

She was small-boned, almost childlike. Murash was very pale, almost sick-looking, and much skinnier than most of us. We might be starving soon, but Murash looked as if she had already been malnourished when she went into hibo.

"You must have some idea," I said. "You came here in your little spacecraft, you docked with us. When did that happen?"

"A long time ago."

Sacer leaned in. "That's the best you've got?"

"There is a clock on the capsule. It has been counting since launch. If it is still working, it will say for how long I have been docked. You have seen my capsule, or you would not be looking for me. Were the systems still working?"

Yesli looked at the rest of us before answering. "It seemed dead to us, but we'll have to look at it in more detail. Did you come from the planet we're orbiting?"

"Yes."

"And you know the name of this planet?" I asked.

Again that withering look. She did not have much

time for my questions. But that was her problem, not mine.

"Answer her," Spry said. "We have limited resources and you're not one of us. Start pissing us off, and we'll drop you out of the airlock."

"You won't," Murash said.

Sacer asked: "Why not?"

"Because in the days that I have been awake I have learned that you know nothing at all. You concern yourselves with finding this man, as if that was going to solve your difficulties. Believe me, it will not. You know nothing at all of why you are here, or what has happened everywhere else. And I know *something*. More than you, anyway. That is why you will not kill me."

"If I were you," I said gently, "I would not be in too much of a hurry to put that theory to the test."

After a moment Murash said: "The world is Tottori. We did not fall so far that we forgot the name of our own planet. Not then, at least. Not when I left."

"Tell us what happened," Yesli said. "Do you remember the war, the ceasefire?"

"Your war? Yes. It was history they taught us in books. Old history. It happened long before I was born."

"Fuck," I said, startling myself.

Murash laughed. "This surprises you?"

— ✶ —

Of course it should not have. I knew we had been displaced in time long enough for Tottori to turn into a frozen world, devoid of civilisation. But that was only an intellectual understanding. It was another thing to have it confirmed by a woman sitting across from me, as if it were the least astonishing fact in her universe.

The worst thing was, I did not think Murash was lying.

— ✶ —

"From the beginning," Spry said. "Everything you know. What happened to us. How you came here. What happened to Tottori."

"Your war ended," Murash said, pausing to clear her throat. "They had a ceasefire, then trials, and then a long reconstruction. It took a generation to start moving on. They knew the war had been a mistake, and that it had ruined hundreds of worlds. They did not want it to happen again."

"Did it?" Sacer asked.

But Spry raised a hand, allowing Murash to continue uninterrupted.

"There was never a war like that again. Difficulties, yes. Some small conflicts within solar systems. But the main peace held. Eight hundred years, it lasted."

I could not help myself. "Until another war?"

"Until *they* came." But now none of us dared break her flow. "No one knew what they were or where they had come from. They seemed uninterested in us—just passing through our little corner of the galaxy. They were like glass."

"Glass?" Yesli asked, as if we might have misheard.

"Sheets of glass. Glass as big as worlds. It was like . . ." Murash scrunched her forehead, as if in sudden sharp physical pain. "Hard to describe. Hard to think about. Glass hinging open, too many folds . . . angles that shouldn't be there. Crystal facets. A constant unfolding. Sheets and sheets, geometries. Colours. Very wrong colours. Wrong geometry. They had no thickness, no dimension. But they moved, they organised. They unfolded. They *became*."

"She's cracked," Sacer whispered. "I say we leave her out as bait for Orvin."

"She's trying to describe something language isn't made to describe," Spry replied. "Something huge and alien. Give her a chance."

"We didn't know if they were many or one," Murash

continued. "If the glass was just the one thing . . . a single intrusion, spread across space. If it was linked or discontinuous. It hurt to see it. It hurt to think about it, later. There was nothing we could do."

"Did it . . . attack you?" I asked.

"We tried to examine it. We feared it. It was bigger than our planet. We didn't know what it wanted . . . whether it wanted anything. We should not have examined it." Murash waited, turning her head to read our expressions. She was taking a sort of cruel enjoyment in our ignorance, our collective fear. How little we truly know. "We had ships. But then the ships stopped working. Small ones, yes. They could still operate. But nothing that could skip. Nothing that could go interstellar. Suddenly there was no way to move between solar systems."

Prad whispered slowly: "I do not quite see how this is possible."

Murash had heard him. "And you think it matters? They were above us. Beyond anything we had. They just made our ships *not work*. And that was that. The start of the collapse of our entire civilisation."

"No more commerce between systems," Yesli said. "I can see that would have been a terrible blow. But the systems always had a lot of autonomy. How could it have been the end?"

"Things had changed since your time," Murash

said. "It was different. The worlds depended on each other. It was a way of keeping peace, of making sure we never had such a war again. But they did more than just take our ships from us. Our planet began to grow colder. We did not realise, to begin with, quite what they had done. It was something to do with our stars. They had made them shine less brightly."

Prad began to speak again. I laid my hand on his arm, none too gently, and whispered: "Later."

"They could change physics," Murash continued. "That was the best explanation anyone had. They could alter physics so our ships no longer worked, and alter physics so our suns did not burn as brightly. Reach into their cores, and make the stars ill. That is why we gave them the name we did."

"Which is?" Spry asked.

"The Sickening."

"But they left," I said. "They're not here now, are they?"

"They left," Murash confirmed. "In ten years, they had come and gone. That is all the time it took. And we struggled on, not quite knowing what had happened. After they had gone, our skipships still did not work, and our suns were still dim. But we could still signal between solar systems, even if we had to do it at the speed of light. Gradually, we learned that no one, no system or world, had gone unaffected. The Sickening had touched us all. Left us all wounded and dying."

— ✹ —

If you were born on *Caprice*, then there has never been a time when you have not known of the Sickening. You heard speak of them in your nurseries, you came to know them from the stories told to you in your cots, to keep you from the path of wrongdoing.

There have always been tales of monsters and dragons. The difference is that you did not stop believing in the Sickening as you turned from childhood. You only learned to think of them with a deeper, cooler, more adult fear. On any given day, you knew that they would probably not return. But always you knew that they were still out there.

Yet that was the first day for us. Until then we had no knowledge of them at all. Not even the faintest suspicion that they were out there, or that they had undone all that was good about the peace that soldiers like me had won, with our bodies and our blood. We had burned our lives for a peace that had held, until the Sickening took it away.

Murash broke our innocence.

— ✖ —

"We must have surprised you," Spry said. "A ghost from the past."

Murash looked unimpressed. "We knew more about skip physics than you did. By the time the Sickening came, it was known that sometimes skips go wrong. Clever people said they understood why." She gave a shrug. "It does not matter now. Your skip took you deeper into the future than most, nearly a thousand years, but we understood that such a thing was possible. You were lucky, though."

Prad laughed. "Lucky?"

"You survived the skip. Usually that is not what happens. The ships come out as wrecks. The crew are corpses. We found many wrecks like that, before the Sickening came. But you were different. You had come a long way, and your ship was still functioning."

"Just barely," Spry said. "We made it into orbit around Tottori, which was always our destination. But the ship was still virtually dead—powered down to the basics, the crew and passengers all in hibo. Many of us didn't make it."

"I know," Murash answered. "I am just saying, you can still count yourselves lucky."

"You detected our arrival," I said.

"We were still listening for signals, still watching space for the Sickening. We saw you move into orbit and we recognised you for what you were. A very large ship from the distant past." Murash looked down at her hands. "You were useful to us. We had lost a great deal, in the years since the Sickening. There were many medicines and technologies that were lost to us." She gave a defiant look. "It was not that we were ignorant, just that we had lost the means to make and repair complex things. But we thought you might have some of those things on your ship."

"You say the Sickening made your suns turn cold," Prad said.

"That is true."

"We know about your ice age. But Tottori's sun is only a little cooler than the records say it should be. Whatever the Sickening did, it must be wearing off— your sun returning to its normal temperature, your planet coming out of its ice age. That means there's a chance for all of us."

"Is there?" Murash asked.

"Your planet can recover, rebuild its civilisation— emerge from the cold. And if the Sickening isn't affecting the stars any more, then perhaps we can still use our skipdrive. It got us here, didn't it?"

"Let's not run before we can walk," Spry said.

"Maybe your ship will work," Murash said. "But there is nothing out there. Only more death. Only more cold."

"If things are that hopeless," Sacer said, "why did you bother trying to reach us?"

"What else could we do?" But Murash added: "It was hard—much harder than we ever thought it would be. Space travel had ended before I was born. No one went into space, no one came back. But we still had the knowledge to construct a craft with the capability of reaching your vessel. A chemical rocket, very simple. Even then, there were many who did not think it was worth the trouble. Times were hard enough as it was—not enough food, not enough power. Why squander what we had on a thousand to one chance? But we did it anyway."

"Did you volunteer?" I asked.

"I was selected for the mission. I was small and strong and clever. They taught me your way of speaking, your customs. I had trained for it since childhood. It has always been the biggest thing in my life."

I shivered at the magnitude of what Murash had been asked to do. It was clear to me that she had never had the slightest choice about her fate. She had been shaped for this one purpose, engineered like a tool to do one thing and do it properly.

"What was the plan?"

"To reach your ship, to board it, to explore and document its contents. Make contact with the crew, if possible. Recover medicines and supplies, and send them down to Tottori using your own re-entry vehicles. Fill the capsule with what I could, refuel it from your own stores, and then return."

"What went wrong?" Spry asked.

Murash gave a dry, humourless laugh. "Easier to say what went right. The rocket worked. We launched from the equator. The rendezvous calculations were difficult. You were in a high orbit, and there was only just enough fuel to reach you. But I did it. I identified the design of your ship from our records, found a working airlock. The airlock adaptor functioned as we had hoped. I moved into your ship. It was cold, very cold, but the air was breathable. After that, nothing went well."

"I know that feeling," Prad whispered.

"You were all still in hibernation. Your ship was so damaged there were parts I could not enter. I tried to wake you, but the systems would not respond to me. I tried to find medical supplies, food and water. I tried to find fuel, so that I could make my return trip. I tried to find a lifeboat or escape pod. I found none of these things. I wondered what kind of ship I had found. Now I know."

."Small wonder you didn't want to be found," Yesli said.

"You started trying to kill each other. I knew what you would do to me, if you learned."

"Did you kill someone to get into hibo?" Sacer asked.

"There was no need. I found an empty hibo capsule and eventually made it accept me. I had been trained to recognise your technology, but it still took six weeks. I had used all my food and water by then. I was close to death."

"You look it," Spry said.

"So will you, eventually. Soon you will be down to your last drop of water as well."

"I think we will last a bit more than six weeks," Yesli said. "The ship isn't as dead as when you came aboard. Prad and the others have made a lot of the systems work again. There's no reason why it can't keep us alive for years, if we ration things carefully. And we do have medicine: you just didn't get to it in time."

"Good for us that she didn't," I said. "She'd have sent it back down to Tottori, for all the good it would have done them. Have you seen your world, Murash? Do you know what's come of it?"

She nodded at a window. "I have eyes."

"What do you think happened to your culture?" I

asked. "Did no one think to build a second rocket, to come after you?"

"I told you that times were already hard. There was one rocket. That was all we could do. I signalled back down to the surface, during the weeks that I was aboard. I told them what I had found, and that I could not return. They said that I had been courageous, to have come this far. But I knew that I had failed my world in its most desperate hour." Murash was looking at me directly now, daring me to break her gaze. "I knew they would not last long, after I went into hibo. It was bad enough when I left. Each winter worse than the last, until we had no other season but winter. Perhaps if I found the right things, it might have made a difference."

"I'm sorry that you failed," I told her. "Sorry for your planet, as well. But your mission wasn't worthless. You've already told us more than we could ever have learned for ourselves. That's invaluable. And you're one of us now. You won't be punished for hiding from us—it was an understandable reaction."

"Very good of you, Scur, to presume to speak for the Trinity," Sacer said.

"You're welcome," I said, blunting her sarcasm.

Spry coughed gently. "Scur has only stated the obvious. You'll be treated the same as the rest of us, Murash. The same privileges, the same rations and duties. The same degree of protection—we don't want you hurt, or intimidated, for what you are. You can't go back to Tottori—that's clear enough. But if you accept our terms, you can find a life here, on *Caprice*."

"They will return," Murash said quietly.

"They?" Yesli asked.

"The Sickening. They have gone, but they have not forgotten us. We are nothing to them now—not even a nuisance. So our star warms up again, our world comes out of its freeze. It means nothing. They will return."

"Then we had better be ready the second time," I said.

Murash laughed again. I understood then that there was a kind of desolate hopelessness beyond anything we had experienced so far. Worse than this was the realisation that Murash had a much better perspective on things than the rest of us—that she was much better placed to judge our chances.

"You don't know us," I said. "You think you do, but you don't. We've come through a lot, all of us. The war you only read about in books. We lived through that. It burned us. But we came out the other side. Stronger, sometimes. Always changed. And this is just . . . something else to deal with. You think we're doomed?" I did not wait for her answer. "Fine: put yourself on zero rations until you die. If you can't take the slow way out, there are energy pistols and airlocks. But you won't, will you? You're a survivor like the rest of us. And you know deep down that there's a chance. If you didn't, you would have just killed yourself by now."

"Maybe I have not had the chance," Murash said. But there was a little less spite in her voice than before. After a silence she added: "I want to see Tottori. Properly—not from one of these little windows."

"There's nothing," Spry said warningly. "Just ice."

Murash shook her head. "I saw something. Maybe you were not looking closely enough."

— ✕ —

We had seen an ice-locked world where there ought to have been a bright hub of civilisation and commerce. No stations, no cities, no spaceports—no sign of any industrial activity at all.

But Murash was correct. With our other preoccupations, we had not looked closely enough.

And it turned out that there was still life on Tottori. The ice age had changed the world almost beyond recognition, made our old maps useless, but Murash had known this planet as the great winter closed in, and she knew where her people had moved to, in their last retreat to the equator.

"There," she said, directing our attention to a stretch of coastline as yet uncovered by ice. "In that bay was Skilmer, one of our largest cities. We made parts for the rocket there—the alloys and guidance system."

"There's nothing," Sacer said.

But Yesli's eyes were sharper. "No—Murash is right. There's definitely something there. A community, settlement of some sort. I can see a bridge across that inlet, and those look like smoke trails."

"Why didn't we see it before?" I asked.

"Cloud cover, I suppose," Spry said. "That, and we hadn't lowered our expectations far enough. It's barely a town, let alone a city."

Murash directed our attention a little to the north and a little to the east. "That would be Uskeram. It was always smaller than Skilmer. But I think there are people there. That curving line that projects into the bay—it can only be a harbour wall."

"Then those must be boats," Yesli said.

Needless to say, even with the damaged condition of *Caprice*, it was not hard to turn magnifying instruments onto these putative communities. We had nothing good enough to look at them in detail, but it was sufficient to vindicate Murash. There were indeed towns down on the surface of Tottori—albeit at a level of technological development far below that necessary to make a rocket, let alone a skipship. We saw winding streets, buildings of stone and wood and thatch, many fires and plumes of smoke. We saw animals harnessed for work, drawing loads along icy, rutted roads. We saw sailing vessels in the shelter of the harbour, while the sea seethed grey and cold beyond. No machines, no electricity, no power beyond the energy provided by the burning of wood. There were still forests at the equator, but even from orbit they looked thin and depleted.

In our orbits we mapped other communities. Some of these Murash was able to name, but not all were known to her. Much time had obviously passed since her departure. This world, in its way, was as strange to her as Tottori had been to us when we arrived.

We estimated a total planetary population of around fifty million people.

"Do you want to return to them?" Spry asked.

She looked at him sharply, as if the question might be a trap. "Could I?"

Spry continued: "We don't have a shuttle—nothing that can land on Tottori and then get back to us. The best we could offer would be a one-way trip in one of our pods. We could drop you back down there."

"In Skilmer, or one of the other towns?"

"It couldn't be guaranteed," Prad said. "There's no manual flight control once you hit the atmosphere. The pod would home in on a NavNet transponder, given the choice, but since there aren't any . . ." He bit his lip. "There'd be a large margin of error. That's not really the point, though, is it? For all we know, it's been another thousand years since you docked with us! You had to learn our language from books. What good will you be down on Tottori, after all this time? You'll be as unfamiliar to them as any of us."

"It is still Tottori," Murash answered. "It is still my world, my home."

"They're dying down there," I said. "It's obvious, isn't it? Either dying, or they've been on the brink of extinction and now they're trying to claw something back. But it's still fragile. How long do you think those forests will last?"

"It's not our concern," Sacer said. "If they had something we could use, I'd say we send down Murash as our negotiator. But they're in the stone age. There's nothing we can do for them, and nothing they can do for us."

I squared off against her. "Leave them to their fate—that's what you're saying?"

"Their fate is none of our business. Look, they've managed without us so far. Isn't that enough?"

"They wouldn't have sent Murash if they didn't need help," Yesli said.

"But even Murash would be ancient history to these people. Do you think they even remember sending her? We drop Murash back onto Tottori, what do you think they'll make of her? Even Murash can't say if they speak the same languages she knows."

"I would take that chance," Murash said.

"Right now," I answered, "you're much more valuable to us than you could ever be to those people. I'm not saying we wouldn't help them if it was within our means, but we have to be realistic."

"Now you sound like Sacer," Prad said.

"I'm not. Sacer says we do nothing because these people can't give us anything in return. I say we have nothing to offer them anyway—at least not now, while we're still coming to terms with the condition of the ship. You've said it yourself, Prad: In a thousand days, who knows what we'll have left?"

"Actually, I meant to have a word with you all about the thousand days. It's possible I may be able to buy us quite some more time."

But Prad's face had none of the jubilation I might have expected from this turn of events. Quite the opposite—as if he well knew that the cost he was about to demand of us would be too high.

"You've found a way to stop the memory leak?" I asked, hardly daring to speculate.

"No. Not stop it, or even slow it. The process, as I have said, is mostly random, and I can't get deep enough into the architecture to have much say over that."

"Then I don't see what you can bring us," Spry said.

"It is very simple," Prad answered. "I have been searching the ship for some other substrate that we could use in place of the long-term memory. It has not been easy! The slates are useless—they were designed for pursers and janitors on a luxury starliner! The spacesuits, lifeboats and shuttles are scarcely any better, although they all have a little capacity that we can use. Nonetheless, I have already begun to copy memory sectors into them. It won't make a huge difference to our problem—at best, we may copy between three and four percent of the memory sectors not already overwritten."

I closed my eyes. "That's it? That's the best we've got? Three to four percent?"

"There is something else."

Yesli said: "What?"

"Another form of memory storage, but of a very fragile and highly distributed kind."

I nodded. "Go on."

"The slow bullets. Those of you . . . those of *us* who have them . . ."

"It's all right, Prad. We know you're crew—you don't have to remind us of it every five minutes."

"My point is simply that a majority of the survivors do carry slow bullets. They are not designed for bulk memory storage, but they do have rather a lot of useful capacity. Presently, quite a bit of it is taken up with military-biographical data. You'd be surprised how much."

"So what are you proposing?" Spry asked, while Murash looked on. I wondered how much of the conversation she was following—how clearly she understood our difficulties.

"What I have in mind is rather simple," Prad said. "We replace the data in the bullets with parts of the ship's memory. It wouldn't be difficult. After our search for our friend Murash here, I already know how to talk to the bullets with one of our slates. I can display the information in the bullet, but I can also alter it—erase and replace it. The bullets can be addressed and updated painlessly, without surgery."

I shook my head, thinking of the pictures of my mother and father, tangible links to my old life.

"No. You can't do it this way. The bullets are all we have."

"We must consider this, Scur. While the ship's own

135

memory falls to pieces, we can each of us preserve a part of it inside our own bodies."

"Those of us with slow bullets, you mean."

"There are more slow bullets in the bodies of the frozen dead—enough to go around. We have injectors—you saw one of them when the mob had that man pinned down. There are plenty to go around. The old bullets can be extracted, cleaned of their data and re-implanted in the living." He made an expansive gesture. "I will gladly accept one into myself, for the purposes of solidarity."

"That's very noble of you, Prad."

"Thank you, Scur."

"But you can take your nobility and fuck yourself sideways. What does a bullet mean to you? I'll tell you what it means. Nothing at all. We know what you are, what you were—a fucking *crewmember*."

Something in me had snapped. I could not stop myself.

"I did not mean to trivialise your experience, Scur. I know that you have been in the war . . ."

"You still don't get it, Prad. You never had to fight, never had to take a questionable order, never had to see a friend blown up or wonder if you exceeded your mandate when you met the enemy. You're not a traitor or a war criminal or a civilian black-marketeer. You're a fucking coward of a ship's technician, who was running away from danger when I met him. You were nothing, you *are* nothing."

Prad was looking at me with something between horror and confusion, as if there was a chance this still might prove to be a joke. I knew I had gone too far, been unfair to him. He had not been a coward, just a man trying to survive. What had any of us been trying to do, but that?

Murash looked on with bewilderment and disappointment, as if she expected better of us than this.

But now that I had started, some part of me had to keep going.

"My bullet is all I have, Prad. I wouldn't expect a civilian like you to understand that. You haven't had my life. I should never have been in this fucking war. I was an innocent victim of political corruption. But even then, even after I was conscripted, I did nothing wrong. I followed orders, I gave them, but I never crossed the line. I was a good soldier—*and I should not be on this fucking hellhole of a prison ship.*"

"That's enough, Scur," Yesli said. "Prad was just giving us the options, that's all."

"There aren't any. We don't touch the bullets." And I placed my hand over my chest, as if they might try to take my bullet out of me there and then. "Not now. Not ever."

Prad nodded slowly, raising his hands and backing

away from me as if in surrender. I knew that what I had said could not be easily undone, if it could be undone at all. Perhaps I had done too much damage for that. Prad was the closest person I had found to a friend since the wakening, and I had burned that friendship in a moment's reckless rage.

But I still meant what I had said. My bullet was all that held me to my past. I could not surrender it.

— �֍ —

"We've found him," Yesli said, rousing me from a shallow, troubled sleep.

"Orvin?"

"Who else?" Yesli smiled, and I tried to find the energy to respond. This was how it was going to be from now on, I thought. We would have to take our pleasure in small, petty things, like the capture of a fugitive. The measure of our lives now would not be in how things improved, but in how quickly or slowly they worsened.

"I'm glad."

Yesli added: "He's pretty weak, after all this time on his own, with no food or water. You should see him—make sure he really is the man you say he is."

"There's no doubt."

"All the same, you should be involved in this. We'll have to set an example, of course—do things properly. You've reason to hate him, and so do the rest of us after what happened to Crowl. But we've got to rise above our need for revenge. We'll have to do things with due process, give him a chance to state his side of things . . ." Yesli trailed off, as if she recognised how ridiculous this all sounded.

"It's all right. You can search me for knives."

I ought to have felt jubilant, that we had Orvin back in our care. But so much had changed since he slipped away into the ship. We had learned too much from Murash, and I had been unkind to Prad. All I felt was a kind of empty satisfaction that one task was now completed, and that we could move on to the next.

I washed myself and met Yesli, Spry and Sacer with their new prisoner. It was the same room where we had spoken to Murash, and I had wondered if they might have allowed Murash to be present as well, to offer her outsider's viewpoint. But it was just the four of us, and Orvin. They had tied him to a chair, doubling the restraints. He looked tired, and there were heavy bruises on his face. His eyes were red and puffy, the lids swollen. He seemed to have difficulty focussing.

"There was some resistance," Sacer said.

"I can see."

"Is it definitely Orvin?" Spry asked. "I know he mentioned you by name, before he got away from us. But there could always have been some mistake."

"No," I said, with joyless certainty. "It's him. It's not another man with the same name and it's not someone pretending to be Orvin. This is the man who put a slow bullet into me, set to work its way to my heart, and then left me to die."

"Are you going to argue with her story?" Yesli asked.

Orvin had some trouble answering. He moved to open his lips and spat out a wad of blood and shattered tooth.

"What would be the point?"

"Now would not be the time to test our patience," Spry said.

"Fine then." Orvin gave a sort of defeated sigh. "I met this woman during the war. Whether or not the ceasefire had been declared was an irrelevance. We were in the field of battle, cut off from central authority. She strayed into my sector. I detained her and subjected her to routine questioning, before we were forced to move out."

"That's a fucking lie."

Orvin gave an uninterested shrug. "Prove it."

"Scur doesn't need to prove anything," Spry said. "She warned us you were dangerous and you showed it when you killed Crowl."

Orvin smiled. "So Scur is what she calls herself now? Well, I'm sorry about Crowl. I couldn't help that, though. It was that or face lynch justice."

"Tell that to the mess the auto-surgeon left when it tried to patch up Crowl," Yesli said. "Better still, why don't we let *you* be the one who tests out the auto-surgeon next time? You look like you could use a spell in the surgeon."

"If you want me dead, I can suggest some quicker and easier ways of going about it."

"Is that what you want?" Sacer asked. "Execution? You know, we might actually be able to arrange it. Be easier for the rest of us, not having to share our resources with you."

"Congratulations, in that case. I'll buy you a few days by dying sooner." Orvin forced his puffy-lidded eyes wider, in mock surprise. "Oh, you think I didn't know the state of the ship? You think I'm so stupid that I haven't grasped that we're going to die up here, very slowly, as our systems fail one by one? That there's no possibility of outside help? That the merciful thing would have been for us all to stay in hibo, until the ship rotted around our frozen corpses?"

"We're going to make it," Yesli said. "We have a plan. The ship's damaged, it's true. It's losing memory by the day, by the hour. But it can still keep us alive, and Prad says we may still be able to make a skip, to reach another solar system. We even have a plan to conserve the vital memory sectors. I'm telling you this because I want you to understand that the rest of us have no intention of dying, and we wouldn't be doing you any kind of a favour if we killed you now."

Spry said: "Regardless of your guilt, we can't afford to lose a useful pair of hands. There's work to be done here—unimaginably hard work, and lots of it."

"So the best I can hope for is forced labour?" Orvin laughed, and drooled out another wad of blood and shattered tooth. "You think you can persuade me to do something I don't want to, is that it?"

"I could," Scur said.

He looked at the three members of the Trinity. "Well, Scur—let's call her that—may have a point. If you are serious about not losing a good pair of hands, I'd keep her well away from me. I don't think *justice* is uppermost in her thoughts."

"I'm better than you," I said. "I was during the war, and I am now."

"You think you are," Orvin said. "But if you were alone in this room with me, and I was still tied down, and you had a knife? Or a slow bullet injector, and a slow bullet? Would you be able to stop yourself?" He was looking at me with an almost friendly smile now, thick-lipped and lopsided as it was. "Be honest with yourself, as one soldier to another. We both know what hate feels like. It hasn't gone away just because we spent a little time in hibo. It's like a light filling you up from inside. It's leaking through your skin."

I wanted to deny him, but I knew better than to attempt a lie. It would have been obvious to all concerned.

I so very much wanted to slip a knife into him, between the ribs, and to twist it, and to make him squeal, and to keep him alive for as long as possible while I prolonged the agony. The slow bullet would have been much too civilised for my tastes.

I smiled. "You've got me."

"As long as we're on the same page," Orvin said.

— ✖ —

A little later I met with Yesli and asked her what the Trinity had in mind for Orvin.

"I was concerned that he might turn out to have friends," Yesli said, rubbing at her brow. "Who knows? He's a war criminal by our reckoning, but when you have a ship full of war criminals, that doesn't mean much."

143

"We're not all war criminals."

"I'm sorry." I could tell that Yesli was tired, overburdened with too many new responsibilities and worries. "I just mean, it could have been worse. But there's no support for Orvin. Quite the opposite. Poor Crowl had his friends, and even those of us who didn't know him very well remember what happened in the auto-surgeon. That debt has to be paid, is the feeling. While it isn't, there's a sense of unfinished business."

"Spry seems to think otherwise. He said we couldn't lose another pair of hands."

"Well, there's another way of looking at that. It's true that Orvin can still be of use to us, in the conserving of the memory."

"Go on."

"After his execution, we can skin him. Make paper from his flesh, ink from his blood. I'd even let you make the first cut, if it meant that much to you."

I shook my head. "That wouldn't work for me."

"Too macabre?"

"Too easy. He'd be dead already."

— ✖ —

The trouble started with an argument between two adjoining work parties, over who had claim to one section of the wall. The argument turned violent, and then spread to nearby parties. It became a confused, confined brawl, and it packed the corridors so tightly that it was many minutes before any of the Trinity's peacekeepers had a chance to break things up. Prad and his people did their best to stop it reaching further, by closing internal doors and turning corridors dark. But by then blood had been spilled. By its nature, any tool sharp enough to mark metal was also sharp enough to cut flesh. There were stabbings and gougings. Someone lost an eye.

After the brawl had been cleared, and the mess cleaned up, I went with Yesli to see what all the fuss had been about.

"I don't know why they would fight over a wall," Yesli was saying. "We've barely touched the ship! Why would they fight now, when almost all the walls are still blank? Leave the fighting until we're down to the last corner!"

"That's why," I said.

The words had been scratched shallowly into the metal, passage after passage running along six or seven metres of wall. The scratched letters gleamed with a hard silver purity. It was done quite neatly—

better than some of the mandatory texts—but the work still betrayed the evidence of several different hands having taken their turn.

"This is free inscription work," Yesli said, frowning. "I don't recognise the words, but—"

"I do," I answered. "This is the start of the Book. Our Book—the one read by the people of the Peripheral Systems."

"Are you sure?"

"I know these words, Yesli. I grew up with them."

"I didn't have you down as a staunch believer, Scur."

"I'm not. But my parents both were." I waited a moment. "I spoke to Prad about this. He told me that there were no copies of the Book in the shipboard memory. They'd been lost to the corruption."

"Did you believe him?"

"I think so." But the tone of her question left me unsettled. "You're saying Prad lied? That the Books—ours or theirs—are still in the memory?"

"I doubt that the Books have survived. But I think Prad or one of the other technicians may have been responsible for their deletion." Yesli paused. "He wasn't ordered to do that, but I can't say I'd have disagreed with his decision. Whoever did it, it was the right thing. The Books are too divisive." She looked at me sharply. "You see that, don't you?

These people wouldn't have come to blows over some poetry or scientific knowledge. They came to blows over the Book. Your side, their side—their stupid differences of interpretation."

"The Book is beautiful, Yesli."

"But it will kill us. Yours or theirs—makes no difference. The knowledge has to go. We can't save it. We'll be making a terrible mistake if we do."

"Someone committed these words to memory," I said. "Who knows, maybe the whole thing. I learned passages, parables, but there are people who made it a life's work to know the entire Book."

"I'm not saying it isn't a wonderful act of devotion. It is. And I'm sure there is tremendous grace and power in these words. Tremendous wisdom and humanity—as well as ignorance and superstition and foolhardiness. All that's the best and worst in us. But that doesn't change anything. Someone lost an eye over this, Scur! We've a chance to put these divisive words behind us now—why in all the worlds wouldn't we?"

"What are you proposing?"

Yesli rubbed a finger along the bright-cut inscriptions. "These words aren't scratched very deeply. They can be polished out, the wall made new."

"And the people who did this?"

"They'll be warned against doing it again, but I

doubt that we'll push for any actual punishment." She took a step back, touched a finger to her chin like an art critic at a gallery. "These inscriptions are very well done, aren't they? We couldn't afford to lose good scribers like these."

"They won't let go of their beliefs that easily."

"They will if we make them," Yesli said.

Half a day later the Trinity issued an edict. The inscribing of religious content was expressly forbidden unless otherwise authorised as part of the mandated texts. No one was to use their free inscriptions for this purpose. If they were caught doing so, they would be compelled to polish the walls back to their former blankness, on top of their normal allocation of mandatory texts. There would be no exceptions, no favour given to the people of one Book over the other.

I do not know what Spry, Yesli and Sacer expected of this decree. Meek obedience? If so they did not properly grasp the extent to which the Book permeated the narrow little lives of grunts like me. I was surprised by Spry in particular. The war had taken him too far above the common soldiery.

It was a serious error of judgement.

The hunt for Orvin had united us, temporarily. The search for Murash had offered another focus, and now the scribing provided another. These distractions had been sufficient to make women and men of different allegiances work together, or at least tolerate each other's company. Allies and enemies, friends and criminals—soldiers and civilians. We had found cause to put our differences and suspicions behind us, for the moment.

The Trinity's edict ripped things wide open again.

It began with work teams refusing to scribe the mandated texts. An hour here, an hour there, might not have made very much difference. But a whole lost day was a thousandth part of the time left for us. Of the knowledge we might yet save, a thousandth part was now gone for all eternity.

If it had gone no further than lost work, negotiation and reasoned persuasion might still have saved the day.

It did not stop. Violence broke out again: much worse than before, and spread across much more of the ship. Believers against believers, unbelievers against the faithful. Grudge-settling for the sake of it. I was shocked by my own naïvety, imagining that the worst of these enmities were behind us.

I was wrong about that.

— ✖ —

After the first death I knew what I had to do. It might not make a difference, but it was the only option open to me.

"I need your help," I told Prad.

"So we are speaking again."

"I'm sorry about what I said. It was unwarranted. It was just . . . anger. I had to lash out at someone. You just happened to be nearest."

"There was truth in what you said, though. We aren't the same. I have known no war."

I nodded at the nearest monitor screen, showing the chaos that had spread through the ship—corridors and halls full of brawling people, the bloodied and slumped forms—unconscious or worse. "You're getting a taste of it now. When this is over, if it's ever over, each and every one of us will be on equal terms."

Prad looked at the screen for a long moment. "They do not seem amenable to negotiation. I see there has been another death, and several serious injuries. At this rate we will butcher ourselves by the end of the day."

"Do you have a slate?"

"Of course."

"We need to get to the main cargo bay, where you first told us about the memory loss. Spry and the others are just about keeping order there."

"What do you have in mind, Scur?"

"You know exactly what I have in mind."

It was difficult, making our way through the ship. Without Prad I do not think we could have done it at all. But Prad still knew more of *Caprice* than I expected to learn in a lifetime. It amazed me that there were corridors and service shafts still completely empty of people, their routes and access points known only to the technical staff.

The bay was full of people, and the atmosphere was ugly. No one was actually trying to kill anyone else, though, which was an improvement on the rest of the ship. If there was a chance of turning the tide, this was the only place where it would happen.

Yesli saw me arrive with Prad. The Trinity members and their peacekeepers were at the middle of the mob, holding a fragile order. We had to push our way through, ignoring the shouts and jostles of those around us.

"Forget it, Scur," Yesli said. "They may have bought the idea of blowing up the ship once, but they won't fall for it twice."

"I know, and I wouldn't dream of trying it again." I looked sharply at Yesli. "I could have told you that order would get us into trouble."

"We had no choice," Spry said. He had to raise his voice above the shouting. "Our differences will kill us. We couldn't allow either Book to become a point of division: we've enough reason to hate and distrust each other already."

"The decree has been issued," Sacer said. "If we go back on it now, we'll look weak."

"I'm not asking you to. Let me talk to them."

Sacer laughed at my presumption. "What do you think you have to offer, that we haven't already proposed?"

"My past," I said.

I presented myself to the mob—there was no other word for it. Then I touched my chest, held my fist above the point where my slow bullet was sitting.

Next to me Prad held the slate aloft. He tilted it so that everyone had a chance of viewing its contents.

There was something happening here. It was enough to lower the shouting and arguing by a fraction. Now the mob's focus was on me, rather than the Trinity.

"You know me," I said. "I am Scur. I was a soldier, the same as most of you. I either fought with you or fought against you—if any of that matters now." I waited, allowing the mob to quieten even further. I did not doubt for a moment that my hold on their attention was tenuous. I had to make every word count. "I read the Book, too," I continued. "It meant a great deal to my parents. I wasn't much of a believer, not really. But the words were still a comfort to me during the war, when I was torn away from my home and family. Some of you will know my story, too. You'll know of the trouble I had with Orvin, but that was only a part of it. I was never meant to be conscripted, but it happened anyway. And I tried to be a good soldier. I tried to obey the laws of war, to do the right thing. They taught us to hate the enemy, and I suppose I did. But my parents had always told me that they read about the same prophets we did. That tempered my hate. I knew, deep down, that we were not all that different. And I never liked killing." I cast a glance at Prad, and Prad looked back at me with a questioning eye, asking that I reaffirm my readiness.

"This is my old life," I said. "These people were my parents. I loved them, and they loved me. These words are all that bind me to my home, to the person I was, the world I knew—the faith I was born into. And I give them up now. I am surrendering myself. From this moment, all that I was before the wakening ceases to matter. I'll carry it in myself, but I won't be able to prove a word of it. I could be as good as the best of us, as bad as the worst." I swallowed, gave a nod to Prad. "Do it. And tell them what's happening."

Prad touched something on the slate. He raised his own high, quavering voice.

153

"I am erasing the contents of Scur's slow bullet. She is giving up that part of herself. She is surrendering the means to prove who she was, what part she played in the war."

One by one, the lines of text were vanishing from the slate's screen. The images of my parents lingered for a few moments, then grew cloudy and drained of colour, as if seen through a window that needed cleaning. Then they disappeared completely.

"The process is irrevocable," Prad told our audience. "I am deleting this knowledge at a very deep level, beyond any chance of recovery. And when the deletion is complete, I will overwrite the empty memory sectors with vital data from the ship. Scur will carry a little part of our knowledge within herself, safeguarding it against the failure of the main memory. Scur has already made her choice of what that knowledge will be. Will you tell them?"

"The war poet Giresun," I said. "Her works, all those that have survived until now."

"Giresun was born on one of our worlds, not yours," Spry said.

"I know."

"And yet you choose to conserve her works, over those of one of your own war poets?"

"Someone has to do it."

Spry nodded thoughtfully. "Thank you, Scur. That you should choose to do this . . ."

"She doesn't want it to stop with her," Yesli said. "Do you, Scur?"

"No, I don't." And I turned to Prad. "This man was right. Those of us with slow bullets, we have the chance to make a difference. But we have to give up what we are. We have to sever ourselves from the past. From everything that mattered to us once, everything that made us what we are. We have to let that go."

"The bad among us will get to start afresh," Spry said. "All sins forgotten."

"Whatever each of us is, whatever each of us was, we'll still carry that personal knowledge," I said. "That goes for all of us: the good as well as the bad, and all the shades in between."

"You won't erase the memory of a war that easily," Sacer said.

"I know. But the bullets are a link to what we were. If we cut that link, then at least we've made a start."

"It won't be easy," Yesli said.

"Do you imagine what I just did was *easy*?"

But Prad held up his hand again. "What I have done for Scur, I can do for any one of us. It's simple and quick." And he brandished the slate like a trophy, holding it high above his head. "Scur has chosen to take Giresun's words into herself. She has become Giresun's custodian! Each and every one of us can make a similar sacrifice and a similar choice."

"It needn't just be the soldiers," I said. "There are more slow bullets on the ship—they just need to be extracted from the dead sleepers. But we can do that. The bullets can find new homes—new custodians. Each of us can carry a piece of the past into the future. It just won't be *our* pasts."

"The scribing will continue," Prad said. "That doesn't stop. It can't stop. But the bullets buy us a little more time, and the chance to save a little more information. Better than that, it becomes personal. We'll each carry something unique."

I took a deep breath. I still felt the same. The bullet was still inside me, and I had no objective sense that anything had changed. But my past was falling away from me by the second. I was free of it, for better or for worse.

It was a terrifying, wonderful feeling. Like falling and soaring at the same time.

"If each of us values the total sum of our knowledge," I said, "then each of us will have no choice but to work together to safeguard the entire population of the ship. We have to help each other to live. We haven't time for anything else. We haven't time for hate or bitterness or recrimination or vengeance. All our old lives ended when the skip went wrong. All our new lives began with the wakening." I allowed a silence, surveying the faces before me, trying to judge whether I had made my point or succeeded only in aggravating matters further.

I had to know.

But there was only one way to be sure.

"Who's next?"

"I'll do it," Spry said, touching a fist to his chest. "I'll be the second."

"Are you sure of this?" Prad asked.

"Do it now," Spry affirmed. "Clean my bullet. Before I change my mind."

— �֊ —

There is a lot more that I would like to say about those times. But lately I have been finding the cutting harder than before. I make errors, which require hours of correction. The letters squirm and dance before my eyes. And there is a pain that never quite leaves me.

They say brevity is a virtue, anyway.

— ✖ —

The temptation is to say that my gesture had an immediate and calming effect, bringing order where there had been chaos; instilling good sense and generosity where there had been spite and recklessness. That, within an hour of my statement, the citizens were lining up to have their bullets cleaned.

But that is not how it happened. It took three days for something approaching stability to return to the ship, and even then there were continuing outbreaks of violence. After the violence, we were left with a slow simmering tension that would be with us for years. We called it the "new peace" but it was a peace in only the most fragile of senses. When the worst of the trouble was behind us, we had six dead bodies and many injured.

Eleven of the wounded required the attention of the auto-surgeon. Fortunately it worked better than it had with Crowl, although I was very glad not to be among the first to test it.

They came forward in ones and twos to begin with, to give up the contents of their bullets. Then threes and fours, and then Prad was faced with so many that it was more than he could cope with alone, and so the work had to be delegated, which took even more time.

Some went along with it because they understood my gesture and realised that by surrendering our private pasts, we were contributing to the greater good of the many. I was with Prad during many of the sessions and saw a different species of sorrow on each face. Giving up the past was a kind of grief, and for some it was almost more than they could stand.

Others were a little too eager. We did not review the contents of their bullets before they were cleaned, but I wondered what it was that they were so keen to see deleted.

Perhaps I was misjudging them. Perhaps they were just genuinely grateful to be able to make a valuable sacrifice. I tried to clean my own memory of these faces. I did not want to remember who had been too willing, too anxious to be absolved of the past.

I had been careful in my choice of the war poet Giresun. I knew she was prized by the enemy, and that my adoption of her work would be a powerful conciliatory gesture. In that sense, the decision was as ruthless as it was pragmatic. Many of the volunteers had their own ideas about their choice of custodianship. For the most part, there was no need to quibble with these selections. If the bullet allowed it, the data would be recorded. Others had no strong notion of what would be written into their bullets.

The Trinity's committees were always able to help at that point.

I do not remember when the first skin markings began to appear, but it must have been within the first few months of the new peace. The idea was simple. Whatever knowledge the bullet contained, this would be reflected on the outside, in the living skin of the custodian. It made a perfect symmetrical sense. We would end up inscribing every available surface of the ship, so why not extend that thoroughness to our own bodies as well? I had lines of Giresun cut into my arms, my shoulders, across my back. We had no ink, but we did have the auto-surgeon. Its surgical lasers could be tuned to brand tissue as finely as any tattoo. It was painful, even after the anaesthetic wore off. But we wore the pain with pride, for it meant that we had also surrendered our bullets and given something of ourselves to the ship.

After that, there is not much to add.

You may ask of Murash, but there is no need. Her story is elsewhere, in her own hand. I suggest that you read it, if you have not already done so. She was always apart from the rest of us, simply because she had come from somewhere else. But Murash chose to remain with us, and by immersion in our shipboard society she gained a great faculty with our language—this "ancient tongue" that she had learned as a scholar, on her dying world. Murash demanded a bullet of her own, and wore her brands like the rest of us. She told us much of her world, much of the history that we had skipped over—but even then, I do not think she told us everything. That would have taken more than a human lifetime.

It would be remiss of me not to mention Orvin, and my part in his ultimate fate.

Yesli had forewarned me about the Trinity's decision. There was a sort of trial, and a sort of sentencing process, but the outcome had never been in serious doubt. There was no possibility of a man such as Orvin being rehabilitated back into the crew, not after the business with Crowl. Equally, there was no appetite for prolonged incarceration.

Yes, I understood the logic of it perfectly. Orvin had forfeited the right to life on *Caprice*. But his execution could not be framed as revenge for his crimes. Deterrence, yes—but most emphatically not retribution. We were better than that.

Some of us.

When it came to execution, there were many options open to the Trinity. Eventually, after discussion with Prad and the rest of the technicians, they agreed to use one of the vacant hibo capsules. Orvin would be put to sleep painlessly, just as if his body was being put into hibo. When he was unconscious, life support would be removed. After death, his slow bullet would be extracted and his body disposed of.

The Trinity knew that I did not approve of this course of action. But they were adamant that his execution would be managed humanely. It was a mark of the better society we hoped to become.

I understood all that. But I could not let it stand.

Near the time of Orvin's execution, I contrived to find myself alone with Prad.

"There is something very important I want you to do for me."

There was still an awkwardness between us, for all that Prad had mediated in the cleaning of my slow bullet. I had hoped that he had forgiven me for my outburst, while at the same time knowing that it had put something between us that could never be entirely removed.

But I still needed his help.

"It is good to be of use, Scur."

"You deserved better from me, I know. If I could take those words back . . ." I shook my head. "I can't, I know. They'll be there, remembered, long after we've forgotten half the things we want to hold in our memories. But I must still ask something of you. It's about Orvin."

"I am astonished."

"You know what's going to happen to him."

Prad nodded once. "Of course."

"Do you approve?"

"It seems a relatively civilised mode of execution. We've all experienced the transition to unconsciousness in hibo. You could almost say it was pleasant. A sort of irresistible warm drowsiness, closing over you. I suppose you don't think that's quite fitting, given his crimes?"

"You can make doors open and close anywhere on this ship."

"Within reason."

"I want access to his cell. And a slow bullet, and a slow bullet injector. I know you can get me those things."

"You are quite insane, Scur. This is our justice. It is all we have. If we fight it now, what chance will we have when things become really difficult?"

"I want access to his cell," I repeated. "And the bullet, and the injector. That's all."

"They'll kill you." He thought for a second. "They'll kill me."

"They won't," I said, although Prad must have heard the lack of conviction in my voice. "Some sort of punishment, yes. That's very likely—for me, anyway. We can make it seem as if I coerced you. You'll be off the hook."

"With Orvin's blood on my conscience?"

"You don't need to worry about that. And there won't be as much blood as you think."

"You've been thinking this through."

"For a while."

"Is this worth it, Scur? After all you have been through? To throw everything away now, just for vengeance?"

"If I wanted vengeance, I'd have it. Just get me the things I need, and get me into that room."

"Is that all?"

"There's something else. It'll be easy for you to arrange. But we can discuss that later."

If I had needed to use force on Prad, I think I might well have. Not because it would have pleased me, or because I disliked him. But I could not have allowed myself to fail.

But Prad did as I asked. We met in semi-darkness, in one of the corridors that did not yet have full power.

"Here are the things you wished for." Prad pressed a dark bundle into my hand. I felt cloth, the rattle of hard metal things inside. "The bullet is clean and loaded into the injector. I presume that is to your satisfaction?"

"Thank you."

"The external lock to his cell will open in three minutes. Orvin will still not to be able to work the door from inside. The lock will remain open for another five minutes, but you must not seal the door from within the cell. If you do you will find yourself trapped." There was an uneasy silence. "Is five minutes sufficient for your purposes?"

"I should think so. You've done well, Prad. I'm grateful." I allowed a silence of my own. "You can go, if you wish."

"I think I would rather remain. If you can provide some evidence of coercion, I think that would be appreciated."

"Wait a moment."

I swung the bundle at him, judging the strength and direction of the swing such that it was likely to inflict a bruise, rather than a concussion. Since I could only see Prad indistinctly there was of necessity an element of guesswork involved. The bundle found the hard edge of a cheekbone or jaw. Prad grunted and slumped into the side of the wall.

There was a silence.

I feared for a moment that I had put too much enthusiasm into my swing.

"Prad?"

There was a groan. I sensed his form next to me, regaining his balance. I heard the scrape of hand against skin, tracing the extent of what would soon be a most impressive bruise.

"Most commendable, Scur. You should consider a career involving violence. I believe you have an aptitude for it."

"I have a knife," I said. "I'm going to keep it between us, just for show."

— ✳ —

We reached the cell. Since the automatic door was presumed to be infallible, there had been no need to station a guard outside. I had counted on this—I saw no reason for the Trinity to have taken unreasonable precautions—but it was gladdening not to be proved wrong.

"You've come this far," I whispered to Prad. "No one will disbelieve your story now, if you want to go. This is a very dangerous man."

"That is why I took the additional precaution of including an energy pistol in the bag. I thought one of us might appreciate it."

I shook the bundle open, as quietly as I could. The injector came with its own pressure line and pneumatic reservoir. I untangled the parts and satisfied myself that the injector was of the design I knew from my military career. It was all there—including the chambered bullet. I also inspected the little standard-issue shipboard energy pistol, recognising it from the time Prad and I had first met.

"Take it," I told Prad.

He closed his hand around the contoured grip. "The yield is set to debilitate, rather than kill. I think you will find the injector in perfect order. You neglected to mention the need for an anaesthetic preparation, so I did not provide one."

"Very thoughtful of you." Now that I had examined it, I slipped the injector back into the bundle, out of sight. "How much time do we have?"

"About four minutes now."

"Let's wake our baby."

But in fact Orvin was already awake when we opened the door to his cell. It slid aside, recessing into the wall. He must have heard our voices or our approach, for all that we had tried to be as silent as possible.

A nervous man, awaiting a visit from his executioners.

Fully dressed, he moved to raise himself from his bunk. On his face was an almost amiable expression, as if I were an old friend paying him a surprise visit.

"Well, Scur. Who did you bribe—or fuck—to make this happen? No, let's stick with bribe. You're not worth that much trouble to anyone."

"Shoot him."

Prad levelled the energy pistol, squeezed off a single discharge. Even though I was nowhere near the direction of his aim, I still felt a sort of shivery tingle run through my nervous system.

Orvin collapsed back onto his bunk. His eyes were still following me, but the energy pulse had winded him. He moved his jaw, trying to make sounds come out.

"It was a mistake," I said.

He croaked out: "What?"

"Choosing me, back in the bunker. You should have found another victim. Or at least stayed to finish the job."

Some of the fight was coming back into him. I glanced at Prad, making sure he was ready with the pistol if it came to that. "I meant to ask," Orvin said. "How *did* you get out of there?"

"I cut the bullet out with your knife."

"Really?"

"It didn't want to be cut out. I had to go pretty deep."

"You were lucky to live."

"I must have bled out some. Also, it wasn't what you'd call a sterile surgical environment. I'd have probably died in there, even with the bullet out of me, if the peacekeepers hadn't swept through. I owe them everything."

"Even after they put you on a prison ship?"

"We both know how that feels. Still. I'm alive, aren't I? That has to count for something."

"This isn't the happily ever after we were hoping for. We fought the war, Scur. Did our duties. We were due our reward."

"The reward is not being dead, Orvin. Or crippled, or in agony for the rest of your life. I'll take being alive."

"Under these circumstances?"

"We've got a ship, a purpose. We'll try a skip soon, see what else is out there. We can live on this thing, until we think of something better."

"It's the end of everything. You think we'll make the slightest difference?"

"We can," I said. "We've already begun to preserve what we can—cut it into our flesh, into the flesh of the ship. Now we have to start putting that wisdom to good effect. It's not much, I grant you. But we've got the benefit of hindsight. We know our history— what worked, what didn't work. If people survived the Sickening on Tottori, then they survived else- where. We'll find them. We can start saving these worlds, a planet at a time."

"Good luck with that."

I removed the injector from its bundle, giving Orvin plenty of time to recognise it, and see that it was intact and came with all the necessary elements.

"No," I said. "I'm not the one who needs luck today."

"Ah, I see. An eye for an eye. The appetiser before the main dish of my execution. Well, be careful. You wouldn't want me to die before they put me into hibo."

"As if I cared." I smiled. "But actually, I do care. That's why the injector and its bullet are properly sterile, unlike the thing you put into me. I'm not going to let infection be the thing that eases you out of this. Oh, and I've never really believed in an eye for an eye." I hoisted the injector by its grip, curling my fingers around the bulky trigger. "But there *is* a certain justice in it, I suppose. Can you guess what's going to happen now?"

"You're going to do to me what I did to you."

I allowed him a good look at the injector. "Standard issue, Orvin. Not modified in any way."

"And the bullet?"

"That would be telling. We wouldn't want to spoil all the fun, would we?"

Still holding the injector, I used the knife in my other hand to slit the fabric of his trousers a little above the knee. I pushed the injector against the skin, until the nozzle had almost buried itself in his flesh. I drew a breath and squeezed the trigger. I heard the crack and hiss and felt Orvin's leg spasm as the slow bullet was propelled into him. To his credit, he let out only a grunt.

I was sure I had made more noise than that.

"Get this over with, Scur."

"What's the hurry? There was no hurry when it was my turn. You left me with that thing working its way through my leg. I'm sorry about the pain, incidentally."

"Are you really?"

"It's less about revenge, more to do with me wanting you to carry an indelible memory of this procedure. If there was no discomfort, it might easily slip your recollection. And it's very, very important to me that you remember the slow bullet."

"Maybe it slipped your mind, but I'm about to be executed."

"No, you're not. And I don't want you to die of infection, either, which is why I made sure the injector and the bullet were both sterile. Later, you'd better treat the wound with a first aid kit. There'll be one in the capsule. Use it sparingly, though. It'll be all you have."

Orvin narrowed his eyes. He could tell this was not going the way he had expected, but exactly what I had in mind was evidently still a mystery to him.

"What capsule?"

"Yes," Prad said from behind me. "What capsule?"

"The escape pod," I said, twitching my head to address both of them. "The one we're going to put Orvin inside. Silly me, though—I'm getting ahead of myself. Can you feel the bullet's progress, Orvin?"

"What do you think?"

"Unlike the one you put into me, it's not going to kill you. It'll hurt, and it's going to keep on hurting. But it's not going to damage any vital organs or bleed you out. All it's going to do is keep going until it reaches its destination—the core body location where your *other* bullet's already lodged. Then it stops. The entry track will heal. You'll get over the pain, more or less. There'll be no sepsis. But the bullet will be there. In you."

"Why two bullets, Scur?"

"It didn't stop you putting another one into me."

"Ah, but that was pure, unadulterated sadism. You've something else in mind."

"Insurance," I said. "In case the first bullet loses its power, or fails in some way. This one is fresh, since it hasn't been inside you while you were in hibo. It has enough power to last the rest of your life, by a comfortable margin. Wherever you get to, we'll easily find you again."

"Wherever I get to?"

I placed my hand on his shoulder. "Don't get me wrong. You're a piece of dirt, Orvin—the lowest of the low. But you're also a man from the past. You were alive before the Sickening came. That makes you too valuable to execute. Now move."

"What are you doing to me?"

"Giving you the thing you don't deserve," I said. "A second chance. Not much of one, I'll grant. But down on Tottori, they need someone like you more than I need revenge."

"I did not think Scur would do the obvious thing," Prad said, with a wondering tone.

"This is a trick," Orvin said.

I smiled in his face as we pushed him out of the cell, Prad keeping a tight grip on the energy pistol. "The fact is, Orvin, you know stuff. You can't help it. Dregs and scraps of knowledge, it's true. No more than the average sadistic thug. But right here, right now, just being an average sadistic thug puts you centuries ahead of the rest of civilisation—at least on Tottori."

"You're quite mad, Scur."

As we made our way to the escape pod I kept on talking. "I can't promise that you'll end anywhere close to a settlement—not after what Prad told me about the guidance control on these escape vehicles. So you're going to need to button up well and steel yourself for a long hike. But eventually you'll make contact with the locals. You'll figure out the hard stuff for yourself—language, customs, communicable diseases."

"And then?"

"You start making a difference. For the better. You're going to help with medicine, agriculture, basic technology. The ruins are still in place. You can help those people begin to put things back together. You can stop them taking wrong turns. Help them begin to rebuild. Tell them what you are, if you think it'll help. Or make up some other story—say you're a traveller from the south, or a wizard, or whatever you think will work. It's up to you. Be creative."

We had reached the entrance to the escape pod. It was one of a curving row of airlocks, each of which fed a vehicle clamped onto the other side of the hull like a limpet. We would be losing the pod, squandering it on a single occupant. It was only one of many, though, and the sacrifice struck me as acceptable.

I had expected Orvin to resist, as soon as my intention became clear. Prad was ready with the energy pistol, just in case—I had told him to dial up the yield, if he needed to make his point more forcefully. But when Orvin did try and break away from us, the gesture seemed more token than any genuine attempt at escape.

We were giving him a chance at life, when the alternative was recapture and execution.

I shoved him into the capsule, told him to buckle in well. I pointed out the survival rations and first-aid kit, reminding him to treat the wound in his leg. He was breathing rapidly, his face glistening with sweat, his eyes wide. By now the pain must have been excruciating.

He had needed it. It was essential that he remember. A year or ten from now, it would be too easy to allow the knowledge of it to slip from his preoccupations. I wanted the pain of this to burn through the years like hell's own fire.

He could never be allowed to forget.

"I don't know when we'll be back," I told him, when we were ready to seal the door and detach. "I doubt it'll be any time soon. Maybe the skip will kill us. Even if we make it, there are a lot of systems out there we need to visit, and besides—I do need to give you *some* time to make a difference."

"And when you return—if you return—exactly how will you decide whether I've measured up?"

"You'll be called to account, that's all I'm saying. We'll find you easily enough. Give it your best, and you'll be treated fairly. Fail us—fail the world—and it'll be a simple business to tell your bullet to kill you. You wouldn't even need to know that we've returned. We could learn a lot just by looking down from space."

"And what if you don't come back?"

"Then enjoy your old age. Remember, your best chance of survival is to lift that world out of the dark ages. I'd get working on that pretty quickly, if I were you."

"Give me a weapon. Doesn't have to be much."

"You have a weapon," I said, studying the hopeful gleam in his eyes. "It's called fear. It's going to be at your back, every waking hour of your life."

I backed away, exchanged one wordless glance with Orvin, and then sealed the airlock. Prad double-checked the settings displayed on the launch board next to the airlock. The pod's automatic guidance system would home in on Tottori and do its best to drop him on dry land, as close to the equator as possible.

Nothing else was guaranteed.

"You are sure of this, Scur?"

"Perfectly."

I thought of the bullet eating its way through Orvin, the twitch and snag of its tractor grapples and probes. It struck me that I had made him into another kind of slow bullet. I would fire him into the skin of this world and leave him to worm his way to some position of power or influence, however slight.

My plan was not foolproof. Given sufficient shielding, the slow bullet *could* be screened from long-range detection, and similarly isolated from any kill-command. But on Tottori their industrial civilisation had declined to the level of pack animals and sailing ships. Merely to create the necessary screening would compel Orvin to initiate a minor revolution in metallurgical refinement and manufacture.

I would not quibble with that.

By the same token, though lodged deep in his chest, the bullet would not be *entirely* beyond the reach of conventional surgery. But for such a dauntingly ambitious operation to succeed, Orvin would need to advance medicine and anaesthetic control to something close to our own. Orvin could be as self-interested as he wished, provided there were tangible benefits to the rest of the population.

We would see. I cannot say that my hopes were high. But this was our first attempt at resurrecting a world and there were bound to be some miscalculations. Orvin was an unlikely ambassador for a new planetary enlightenment. But if he could make a difference, there was hope for the rest of us.

Not much, perhaps. But I would take what we could get.

I heard a thump, as of a fist on the other side of a heavy metal bulkhead.

I touched the launch control.

There was no countdown, no moment of hesitation before the pod's departure thrusters fired. There was a muffled clunk, like a key turning in a lock, and then silence. Against the vast mass of our ship, we felt nothing of the recoil. But through the adjoining viewports Prad and I watched the little lozenge-shaped capsule tumble rapidly away, our own rotation seeming to curve its trajectory against the planet's white-mantled hemisphere. The thrusters would operate only long enough to carry the pod to the edge of the atmosphere, whereupon it would make a fiery and barely controlled descent to the surface. By the time its scorched shell reached the ground, fuel tanks drained, there would be no possibility of it returning to space.

"Almost until the end, he still thought you were going to kill him," Prad said, when at last we had lost sight of the falling object.

I nodded at the face of the world. "What makes you think this isn't a death sentence?"

"I do not think you have it in you, Scur. You would like to think that you are as capable of cruelty as Orvin, but you are not. You want him to redeem himself, and you want him to help this world."

That was when I heard a set of footsteps, approaching rapidly from both directions.

I still had my knife, and Prad's bruise was looking better by the moment.

"All right," I snarled. "You've done your part."

It was Yesli and Spry coming from one direction, Sacer and Murash from the other.

"What in the worlds . . ." Spry began.

"He's gone," I said. "I let him go."

"No," Sacer said, with a flat certainty. "She couldn't have done this. He's still in his cell. This is some kind of weird bluff."

"I am afraid she is quite sincere," Prad said, caressing his bruised jaw. "I saw everything, as well. She broke Orvin out of confinement, put a slow bullet in him. The pod has already commenced atmospheric entry. It's quite beyond recall now."

"I thought . . ." Yesli started to say.

"You thought what?"

"That you would kill him, given half the chance. Do back to him, what he nearly did to you."

"I did."

"But to different effect," Spry said. "Not to torture him . . . but to make him useful to us. That was your plan, wasn't it?"

I nodded, for there was no point in lying. "Murash knows that world better than any of us. But we couldn't send Murash—she's much too valuable to us up here." I looked at her apologetically, for I knew we would soon be skipping away from this system, away from this home of hers, and there was no guarantee that we would ever return. "I'm sorry, Murash—that's just the way it is. Anyway, you'd be almost as much a stranger to those people as Orvin will be."

Murash's face was stony. I did not know what she liked the least: that she could not go back, or that I had deemed Orvin an acceptable substitute.

A hero for a war criminal. It was not much of a bargain. But I suspected we had harder ones ahead of us.

— ✶ —

Later I was allowed to witness Orvin's passage through the atmosphere, tracked by our sensors. No part of this ship was new, and there had always been some doubt in my mind that the pod would function as it was meant to. But Orvin's landing was entirely within the specified parameters for survivability. Our observations showed that he had come down in an area of forested mountain, now under snow. We had no visual direct acquisition of him, just a bright thermal smudge, the only hot thing in this landscape, but the telemetry from the pod, and the continued functioning of his slow bullet, told us that nothing untoward could have happened.

But for a long hour nothing happened.

The pod was inert, the slow bullet showing no measurable change in location. Perhaps, despite everything, I had been too rash in sending the lifeboat away when Orvin was loose of his restraints. Perhaps, the telemetry notwithstanding, something must have gone wrong—some fault that the pod was too damaged to report.

On the other hand, if it were me in that thing, I would not be in a desperate hurry to leave it. The pod was safe and warm, for now, and I had not lied about the supplies and equipment. Outside was a freezing cold snowscape, a forested wilderness stretching for hundreds of kilometres in all directions. Even with the on-board provisions, crossing that bleak territory on foot would be a particular sort of hell. And beyond it, there was no promise of warmth and light and the nourishments of civilisation. The best our envoy could hope for was something one step up from the dark ages. Cold rooms, dark nights, and lives bent by war, misery, disease and the almost universal prospect of early death. He would be mad to leave the capsule.

But sooner or later he would need to. He could wait until the last moment, when starvation and cold had forced it upon him, or he could do the wise thing and begin his journey immediately, when he was at his strongest and sharpest.

We waited.

Presently Prad drew my attention to a small cluster of moving heat sources, not very far from Orvin's landing zone. The tree cover prevented any clear view of the moving things, but their questing, packlike behaviour left us in no doubt that they were some kind of hunting animal. From above, where we could not see their legs or more than the grossest details of their anatomy, they moved like hot maggots. I thought of something as hardy as a wolf, either a native organism or something imported from Earth. Perhaps the sound of Orvin's arrival had drawn the curiosity of these creatures.

"What are they?" we asked Murash.

"Hungry," she said.

The hot maggots, twenty or so of them, had arrived close to the capsule. A number broke from the main mass and approached the parked vehicle. They circled it, coming closer before darting away and approaching again.

"Movement," Prad declared.

A sudden change in the heat signature of the capsule. Air blushed out of it. Orvin had broken the seal, surrendering his little pocket of warmth.

We watched a smaller blob detach itself from the capsule—cooler than the container it had arrived in. The blob made trudging movements—it was not made for locomotion in this environment. The animals had backed off, but they were not retreating. They formed a pincered crescent, ready to dart for Orvin if he made a dash for the left or right.

For long moments Orvin and the animals stood their mutual ground. Then three of the creatures broke from the centre of the shield and began to advance.

Orvin's blob extended a spiked pseudopod. Heat flashed from the end of the pseudopod.

"You gave him a weapon?" Sacer asked.

"Standard issue energy pistol," Prad answered. "There is always one in the survival pack, although I do not think Orvin would have known until he looked."

One of the animals tipped over. We could see it properly now. It was perfectly still, oozing warmth into its surroundings. The other pair had sprung back. The cordon was breaking up, retreating. Orvin stretched his arm again and fired the pistol a second time.

A second animal dropped.

"Be careful," I whispered to myself. Did he imagine there were additional power cells, somewhere in his supplies? Or was he just applying a calculated reinforcement of his first demonstration, knowing full well that each shot had to count?

The animals, except for the two he had killed, dispersed into the woods. They would regather later, I was sure. But they would take no further interest in this bewildering newcomer.

Orvin moved to the first of the corpses. He seemed to kneel next to it. We had no idea what he was doing, except that it took several minutes and when he was done the animal's warm remains were spread over a larger area. He moved to the second animal, and repeated the same bloody ritual. Then he returned to the capsule. His blob vanished back inside the cooling shell. He was busy for only a few minutes before re-emerging.

He moved between the corpses, then kept going. We tracked his progress for many hours, wondering if he would eventually turn back. When night fell, he stopped and made camp, utilising the thermal sleeping bag we had given him. In the morning, though, he continued on the same course. His progress was exhaustingly slow, but I doubted that I would have been any quicker given the combined difficulty of the terrain and the surface conditions.

"He's going in roughly the right direction," Prad announced, when we had all arrived at much the same conclusion. "Three weeks at this pace, he should make the outskirts of . . . what is the name of that place, Murash?"

"Uskeram," she answered.

"Will they welcome him?"

"In Skilmer we spoke of an Uskeram welcome." She paused. "It was not a good thing."

"If he's careful with the rations, they should see him through," I said, before swinging around to address the individual members of the Trinity. "I'd like to know your plans, if you don't mind. Do you want to stick around until Orvin reaches Uskeram?"

"I would rather not wait three weeks to find out whether or not we have skip capability," Yesli said.

"I agree," Spry said. "Before you sent Orvin down there . . . did you think to tell him when we might return?"

"I said it might be a little while. I don't imagine he will ever stop watching the sky."

"Nervously, I hope," Spry said.

After a silence Yesli said: "Something's happened here, and I'm not sure what. You acted against the wishes of the Trinity, Scur, and that can't be taken lightly."

"I wouldn't expect it to be."

"Equally . . . I'm not even sure this counts as a crime. If it is a crime, I'm not sure we have a word for it."

"She can't go unpunished," Sacer said indignantly.

But Spry met this remark with a dry laugh. "Look around you, Sacer. We've been ripped out of time, thrown into a dark age, told that there's an alien horror out there that will probably come back and kill us. Our ship is half dead and we have a faint chance of saving the tiniest fraction of its memory before it vanishes into oblivion. Some of us are saints and some of us are sinners, and thanks to Scur we have very little idea of who's who any more. This is our own special circle of hell, and it comes with metal walls and a skipdrive that may blow up the instant we test it. Remind me which part of this isn't *already* a punishment?"

"It's all right," I said, grateful for Spry's words but knowing I could not hope to get off quite that lightly. "I know what I did, and I expect to be punished. I broke our laws, but that doesn't mean I don't respect the rule of law."

"Then I might add something," Prad said quietly.

"Go on," Yesli replied.

"It was Scur's wish that I not be implicated in her plot. That is why she struck me, so that it would seem as if she forced me to act against my wishes. But the truth is that once I had some idea of her intentions, I went along with it willingly. And I am proud that I did so."

"Be very careful," Sacer said.

"Oh, I am very careful. Very risk averse, as Scur well knows. But I am proud of this. It was good that we not kill this man, and good that we gave him a chance to do some good himself."

"He won't," Sacer said.

"Perhaps he won't, or perhaps he will. We are all different since the wakening. Who is to say Orvin will not change, given time? At the very least, I do not think it can fail to be an interesting experiment. And it has cost us very little."

"Except a death," Sacer said. "We could have used his skin and blood."

"In the years to come," Prad said, "I doubt that there will be any great shortage of corpses."

Prad had been right about many things. As much as it pains me to report, he was right about that as well.

— ✠ —

There is not much more to say. They never punished me for my one crime, such as it was. I remained a free woman aboard the ship. I broke bread with the best and the worst of my fellow survivors, and I left my share of blood on the walls. It has taken me most of my life to cut these words.

We skipped, and we lived.

A hundred times, a hundred systems. Always knowing that they might be out there somewhere, waiting to poison our stars again, to take our technology away from us.

We have not found them yet. Or been found by them.

And we have raised a hundred worlds from darkness, or tried. I do not doubt that we sometimes did more harm than good—that we prolonged suffering, instead of ending it. But what else could we do? We had nothing to guide us but our instincts. We had no wisdom to draw on but the marks we had made on the walls, back when the world was young. And none of us had been born for this. The war had made us what we were—traitors, cowards, murderers and sadists. We were all dregs of one sort or another. Even the best of us had sometimes lied about what we had done, or how we had found our way aboard *Caprice*.

A year or two before he died, Prad told me that he had found an anomaly in my slow bullet readout. It had been a small thing, easily overlooked. I remember now that he had mentioned corrupted sectors, parity errors. It might have been nothing more than the sort of random corruption that had befallen the bullet during the centuries that we were frozen in hibo.

Or it might have been something else. A sign, perhaps, that the contents of my bullet had been deliberately altered before I ever entered the ship.

That one history had been replaced by another.

I say it is strange because here, now, at the end of my own life—or near it—I cannot say that Prad was wrong or right. I should remember, but I do not. My mother's love of Giresun, my sister Vavarel, my family, my father's sense of honour, my time in the war, my encounter with Orvin. Did all of that happen to me, or did I steal some of it from another soldier? In the chaos of the ceasefire, Prad told me, such things would have been possible. If a bullet can be altered, overwritten now, then it could also have happened back then. If the money was there, and the need sufficient.

Equally, perhaps it was just a random anomaly.

Who can tell?

I say this now because I have nothing to lose. All that I now remember is what I have cut on these walls. These marks are all that define me. If my name is not Scur, then I have certainly *become* Scur. And I have tried to do right by that name.

I mention this now because there will not be another chance. I am going to die—this seems certain— but not for several months. There is something growing in my head that the surgeons cannot fix.

189

It presses on my optic nerve, confuses my seeing. It explains the mistakes I have made in my cutting, the difficulty I have had in focusing.

I have a year, if all goes well. And that is time to make a difference.

In a little while, before we skip again, I will be sent down to another frozen world. There is no chance of my returning, and no chance of the world's medicine doing me any good. Like Orvin, I will have a limited time in which to offer my guidance. Unlike Orvin, who perhaps knew me better than I know myself, I do not expect to be judged for my efforts—at least not while I am alive. But perhaps when you return, you will decide how I have done.

Until then, whoever I was, whatever I did, whoever *you* are, think well of me.

I called myself Scur. I was a soldier in the war.

I set my hand to these words.

ABOUT THE AUTHOR

Alastair Reynolds is the author of eleven novels, including the Revelation Space series, and has also published over fifty short stories.

Reynolds earned a degree in Astronomy from Newcastle and then received a Ph.D. from St. Andrews in Scotland. In 1991, he started a fellowship at the European Space Agency, where his two-year position lasted thirteen years.

The first of his short stories was published in 1990 while he was in graduate school. His first novel, *Revelation Space*, was published in 2000. His second novel, *Chasm City*, won the 2001 British Science Fiction Association Award for Best Novel. His other novels include the Poseidon's Children series. He also has written a Dr. Who tie-in novel, *Harvest of*

Time. Reynolds has earned recognition for many of his novellas and short stories, including the 2010 Sidewise Award for Alternate History for "The Fixation."

Reynolds cites some of his literary influences as Arthur C. Clarke, Isaac Asimov, Larry Niven, Frederik Pohl, Gregory Benford, and Joe Haldeman. His film and television influences include *Doctor Who*, *Star Trek*, *The Time Machine*, *Fantastic Voyage*, and *From Russia with Love*.

Reynolds currently lives with his family in Wales.